Gift

A Journey of Sacrifices

AARYAN BHARGAV

INDIA • SINGAPORE • MALAYSIA

Notion Press

Old No. 38, New No. 6
McNichols Road, Chetpet
Chennai - 600 031

First Published by Notion Press 2018
Copyright © Aaryan Bhargav 2018
All Rights Reserved.

ISBN 978-1-64429-790-2

This book has been published with all efforts taken to make the material error-free after the consent of the author. However, the author and the publisher do not assume and hereby disclaim any liability to any party for any loss, damage, or disruption caused by errors or omissions, whether such errors or omissions result from negligence, accident, or any other cause.

No part of this book may be used, reproduced in any manner whatsoever without written permission from the author, except in the case of brief quotations embodied in critical articles and reviews.

Dedication

Dad, I'm sorry I didn't tell you about this. I never wanted you to freak out. I had left my job a long time ago to pursue my dream, writing stories. It doesn't matter how big or how small I do, I will always do it for you. You are my idol, my inspiration, my hero. Please don't be mad at me.
I love you dad

Contents

Acknowledgements	*vii*
Prologue	*ix*
Chapter 1: The Café	1
Chapter 2: The Love	14
Chapter 3: The Ice Breaker	52
Chapter 4: The Unexpected	60
Chapter 5: The Alcohol	83
Chapter 6: The Change	88
Chapter 7: The Confession	119
Chapter 8: Tulika	143
Chapter 9: The Hospital	164
Chapter 10: The Gift	173

Acknowledgements

Writing a book is much harder than I thought and fortunately I had plenty of people who helped me reach the finish line. Even though I want to, I am limited to my abilities to take everyone's name at once. Yet I will start with two most important women of my life.

There isn't any line invented yet that'll do justice to acknowledge a mother. But I'll try to put everything in one line. Thank you for everything mom. I love you.

A companion is who makes your journey easier and supports you throughout the way. Nandni, thank you for standing by me through thick and thin and helping me get out of the tunnel. I can't thank you enough, baby. Love you.

Ratnu, my brother from another mother, thank you for constantly believing in me and having my back. A big hug.

Vikram, nigga, thank you for spending sleepless nights to discuss the story line. You are an amazing friend. A high five.

ACKNOWLEDGEMENTS

Pratyush, buddy, thank you for going over that manuscript a million times and helping me improvise it. A big hug.

I would also like to thank Venyush, Kaushik, Srikaanth, Srishti, Simmi, Vivek, Bhavesh, Amandeep, Saro, Vikas, Guppi, Jyotsana, Rahul, Anupreet, Vibhor, Sai, Anirudh, Darshil, Dharmil, Bunny, Yadnesh, Kishor, Chetan, Anoop, Malav, Boss, Neele, Bhuppi, Budha, Meenu, Madan, Anish, Sahil, Gaurav, Harshit, Shikhar, Satish, Rajesh, Mohit, Vineet, Ronak. Manvinder, Roshan, Shubham, Sitaram ji, Rohini, Richa, Manish, Vikash, Sumit, Sumit P, Nikhil, Hitesh, Shrey, Aahana, Prateek, Yuvraj, Nysha, Abhijit, Sarang, Rahul, Vipin, Rocky, Sachi, Smikun, Rajdipika, Sonali, Pari, Roma, Anil, Rajat, Abinash, my brother Akash, my uncle, my aunt, my grandma, my grandpa and my cousins- Rinky, Chumu, Raja, Guddu for at one point or the other you guys did stick with me, motivated me and made it sure that I stay on the track.

Finally, I would like to thank my ever-patient publishing manager Gabriela, my editor and my designer. You guys are awesome.

Prologue

6 August, 2018. Fortis Hospital, Navi Mumbai

I was sitting on a bench outside the private ward. I saw a few faces, just like mine, drowned in hopelessness. There was silence. The reticence of grief. Suddenly, lightening streaked through the sky, lighting up the hall I was sitting in. I looked outside as it started to rain. Tiny droplets clung to the glass wall, making the outside world a blur.

While sitting there, I thought to myself about how I had never imagined this moment in my life: The person I loved the most was battling her fate. I could not witness it. I wished I could take all of her pain. If not all, at least some. But I couldn't. Unfortunately—or, should I say, ironically—this world of ours doesn't work that way.

It had been two years, but I still remembered the day as if it were yesterday. I had met her on a flight. She came into my life like a ray of sunshine, bestowing all happiness on me. But, as they say, every good thing has to end some day. Sooner or later. When I looked back, I couldn't believe that she had kept this secret away from me for so long.

Behind closed eyes, I reminisced the beautiful moments I had spent with her. I heard someone calling my name. I wiped away the tears. The nurse was standing in front of me.

"Mr. Bhargav, she is up and she wants to talk to you," the nurse said.

"Okay," I replied as I rubbed my eyes gently. I got up and headed to her ward.

I walked to the door, and peeped through the glass. She was staring at the rain pouring down on the city. Her eyes seemed to look for a silver lining behind the dark clouds. But there weren't any. I noticed that her face had shrunken even more, revealing the curves of her skull. Her dimples had faded into the hollow grooves. Her eyes seemed to pop out of their sockets. Her skin was literally glued to her bones, like wrapper around a chocolate. The size of her finger had scaled down to that of a cigarette. She looked nothing like what she used to. I couldn't stand a moment of seeing her like that. My eyes started to well up. I felt like going away somewhere alone to cry a river. Yet, I put on a fake smile and stepped into the room. She turned to look at me.

"Hey beautiful!" My fake smile became a genuine one.

She smiled slightly.

"How are you feeling?" I asked as I sat down beside her.

She closed her eyes and nodded. That was her way of saying that she was feeling good. I smiled and caressed her hand. I knew she was lying. Deep down, she was scared.

"Look at the rain. It's so beautiful, no?" I said. We both looked at the window.

"I want to go out and dance," she said.

"Me too."

She looked at me with a smile. "Aaryan, open that drawer." She pointed to the drawer next to her.

I opened it. There was something, which seemed to be a gift. There was an envelope as well, placed on it.

"What's this?" I asked her.

"Today I'll tell you a story."

"What story?"

"A story about three people."

"Who are they?"

Prologue

I did not have the slightest idea of what she was talking about, but I sat there and listened to her intently. She started to speak.

Chapter 1

The café

18 January, 2016

"Wake up, Rehan. It's ten already." The loud voice rang in Rehan's ears. His eyes were closed; hands were wrapped around a pillow, head was buried inside another, and legs were sprawled on the bed. He was sleeping like a baby.

It was a wintry morning. Sunlight shone through the window and lit up the room with a soft glow. The white curtains were waving in the breeze. Everything in the room looked serene. The room was decorated in a monochromatic theme—everything was either black or white. From the outside, the room looked like a small piece of black and white heaven.

Tulika was standing in the doorway and looking at Rehan. She was smiling; her eyes gleamed with a strange kind of affection. She was holding an album in one hand and her bag in the other.

"Wake up, Rehan. You don't want to miss this meeting," she said, as she put the album into her bag.

Rehan was still sleeping—as always. Tulika packed her bag, put on her shoes and turned to leave. She shouted again, "Rehaaaaan! Wake up! I'm leaving." She waited at the door for few seconds to hear his response. "Yeah. Okay," came the reply. His voice was slow and sounded grumpy. She smiled and closed the door behind her.

Rehan went back to sleep.

Rehan loved his sleep. If it were up to him, he would never leave his bed. He had the habit of hugging the pillow, as if it were his girlfriend. So much love for the mattress and pillows—his sleeping buddies!

Fifteen minutes later, Rehan heard the alarm ring. He waited for it to stop but it went on and on. As the noise grew louder and more irritating, he pulled the pillows closer and pushed them hard against his ears. He squeezed himself into a fetal position and tried to block out the noise.

"God! That alarm clock just won't shut off!" he thought to himself as he became increasingly frustrated.

He kicked off his blanket and squirmed around in bed.

The sound was unusual for him because he had never set an alarm before. Although he had an alarm clock on his table, it wasn't put to much use. His morning nap was very precious to him—which, by the way, he claimed was very dreamy and beautiful.

Rehan was determined to not lose the battle over his sleep. He remained glued to the bed; he pressed the pillows harder against his ears and kept twisting and turning. But the sound didn't let him sleep.

At last, when the noise became too much to endure, he sat up straight on his bed. His teeth were clenched with anger, and his eyes searched for the damn clock so that he could smash it on the ground. He turned and looked around on his bed but still couldn't find it. Furious, he got up from the bed. He searched the entire room and finally found it sitting on his table. Unfortunately, it wasn't the same clock that had been ringing.

This made him so mad that he turned and tossed things around to find the rogue clock. He searched in his cupboard, drawer, bags, under his bed and up on the shelves. When he finished raiding all these places, he sat on the bed and cradled his head in frustration. Suddenly, he realized that the noise wasn't coming from his room. He got up from the bed and rushed into the room next to his. There it was. The damn clock was right in front of him, on the table. There was a piece of paper by its side. He took the clock, turned it off and slammed it back on the table. He grabbed the paper and read: "Finally, you woke up. Go freshen up now. You don't want to miss the meeting. Prithvi Café at twelve, remember? Breakfast is on the table."

Before going ahead, let us know more about Rehan. A Mumbai-based professional photographer, Rehan Mirza was one of the best in his field. Many high-profile clients asked for him when they needed candid shots. He was often invited to cover important film events and celebrity weddings. He had earned a good name in the last few years—his family was proud of him; he was proud of his success, too. He shared an apartment in Hiranandani with Tulika.

Rehan put the letter back; all his anger melted at the sight of that letter. He looked around the room; it was very neat and clean. He smiled as he remembered how it used to look a few months earlier. Tulika had been a total mess when they started living together. She would put her clothes all over the room, and never arranged the things on the table. Forget about breakfast, she had never made even a cup of tea before.

But it seemed that today was a day full of surprises—she had even prepared breakfast for him. He smiled and ran his fingers over the bed as he left the room to take a shower. He was running late for the meeting.

"Wow!" Rehan said when he tasted the pasta. "Can't believe Tulika made this!" He was surprised. It tasted as delicious as it looked. "When did she start cooking?" He remembered the days when he used to cook and serve her. She never did things like cooking, laundry or grocery shopping. Now, she had started doing all of them. He smiled. He finished his breakfast and put the dishes in the sink. He had a glass of milk before he went into his room to get ready.

He had to reach Prithvi Café before noon. He tried to rush whenever he could in Mumbai traffic. It was a weekday, and he was caught in rush hour. Prithvi was about forty-five minutes away from his place. Meeting clients there, despite the distance, was due to a specific reason. Five years back, when he had landed in Mumbai, he had met his first client there. The meeting had gone really well, and he had landed the job. So, the place earned a special place in his heart. He thought the place was 'lucky' for him, so he continued meeting his clients there. With time, as he got all the jobs, his belief grew stronger. That was one reason.

We, too, have such beliefs in our lives. Don't we?

Another was that he loved the sea. He would finish his meeting, and then go to the beach and sit there till sunset. It gave him a sense of peace.

Rehan was about to reach Prithvi when he got stuck in a horrible traffic jam at Juhu Circle. A bus had shut down in the middle of the road, so things had become pretty ugly. Drivers were honking their horns loudly, which only added to the chaos. Rehan rolled up the window as he could do nothing but sit back and wait for the mess to clear. The cafe was only five hundred meters away from the circle. He thought of walking down, but his car would be left in the middle of the road. He had no choice but to follow the herd. As the cars crawled forward, his phone started ringing. It was Anjali.

Anjali Sharma was the client Rehan was going to meet that day. She was an old college friend, and she was getting married the following month. She wanted Rehan to cover her wedding but he hadn't been her first choice. She didn't even know about Rehan's profession—one of her friends had suggested Rehan's name.

"Hey," Rehan said, as he picked up the phone.

"Hi Rehan," Anjali replied, and then continued, "Listen, I'm sorry. I got caught up in traffic and will probably be late. Will you wait for some time, please?"

Rehan was relieved. He had been preparing to call her and say the exact same thing. Now that Anjali had called him first, he had gained an advantage.

"That's alright. You drive safe and take your time. There's no hurry at all," he said, taking the high road. He didn't mention that he was also stuck in a jam because he didn't want to give away his lack of professionalism.

"Thank you. And hey, I have a friend with me. Do you mind if she joins us?"

"No. No. Not at all."

"Okay. See you in a bit."

"Yeah."

Rehan drove the car slowly. He passed by JALSA, the legendary Amitabh Bachchan's residence. He remembered the last time he had been there. He recalled shaking hands with Mr. Bachchan himself, and seeing Aishwarya Rai face to face. That was a day he would never forget. He smiled as he recollected every single event of that momentous day, and savored the excitement and happiness he had felt.

It took him 15 minutes to reach Prithvi Café. He hurriedly parked the car and rushed into the cafe. He was a regular, so everybody who worked there knew him. As soon as he entered, the cashier greeted him with a smile and said "Hello." Rehan responded with a nod. A waiter showed him to his regular spot—a corner table surrounded by tiny colorful lights. He sat there and ordered a coffee. He was relieved that he had reached before Anjali.

As he waited for his coffee, he looked around. Though it was probably the millionth time he was there, it felt fresh. Just like always. He adored this place. It was an open-air café, decorated with bamboo plants and colorful, ball-shaped fancy light holders hanging from them. The interior was dimly lit and soft music played in the background.

He had gone through two cappuccinos. It had been thirty minutes since he had arrived, but Anjali had not yet made an appearance. He was tired of waiting. So, in the meantime, he decided to call Tulika and tell her about the alarm clock.

He called her.

"Hey!" Tulika said, as she picked up.

"I broke your alarm clock," Rehan said, grinning.

"Really?" she laughed. "Don't worry, I'll buy another one."

"It was a terrible idea, setting up the alarm clock."

Tulika laughed again.

"Did you reach Prithvi on time?" she asked.

"Yes. I'm at Prithvi, waiting for the client."

"Okay. Good luck with your meeting. I got lots of work to do. I'll call you later."

"Okay. And, by the way, the pasta was good."

"Just good? At least learn to appreciate good food, you!"

"Ha-ha."

"Okay, I'll call you later. I've got a ton of work."

"Okay."

He put the phone on the table and picked up the menu card. It was getting very hot outside. He started leafing through the list of beverages. He was mentally marking out the ones he hadn't tried yet when he heard someone calling out to him.

It was Anjali, standing right in front of him. She was wearing a white dress, and had a broad smile on her face. Rehan couldn't help but notice how much thinner she had become. She looked much prettier, too—a sharp contrast to the less good-looking version she had been in college. Rehan smiled. He stood up and offered her a seat.

"It's been so long," he said.

"Yeah, since college," she said.

"How are you?"

"All good with me. Tell me, Rehan, how are you dealing with all this fame in Mumbai?"

"Ha-ha. What fame? I'm just doing my work, that's it," he replied modestly. "What would you like? Coffee or tea?"

"Just a latte."

Rehan called the waiter and told him to bring a latte and a cappuccino—his third coffee within half-an-hour.

"So…you must have met all the Bollywood celebrities. No?" Anjali asked.

"Yeah…most of them. So, what do you do now?"

"Same old job at Microsoft. I saw your photographs on Instagram, by the way. You are awesome."

"Thanks."

"I gotto ask you something." Anjali's expression was curious. "Have you dated any of the actresses?"

"Ha-ha. No!"

They laughed for a bit and then fell silent.

"So, getting married, huh?" Rehan started the conversation again.

"Yeah." She blushed.

"Love? Or arranged?"

"Let's say both."

"Hmmm…interesting."

"You don't take up any work besides the celebrity people, right? I'm a little surprised why you took mine. Honestly, I didn't expect that you'd say 'yes' for it. I was just taking a shot."

"Come on now, Anjali. We are friends. I can do it for a friend—though I will charge a lot more than what I usually charge!" Rehan chuckled. She laughed, too.

"So, where's your friend?" Rehan asked.

"Oh. She is just outside, talking to her mom. She will come in a bit." She pointed to a girl in a yellow dress, who was standing in the parking lot and talking on the phone.

The girl caught Rehan's eye. He kept stealing glances at her. She was facing away from him, and was walking back and forth, so he couldn't see her face. Anjali started talking about her fiancé and how they had met and decided to get married. She excitedly rambled on about her wedding preparations. The words reached Rehan's ears but his brain was too busy dealing with thoughts about the girl in the yellow dress. He would look at Anjali for a moment, listen to her, nod, and then quietly look at the other girl. He kept tapping on the table as he waited for her to turn. Anjali was too caught up in narrating her own story, so she didn't notice Rehan's impatient behavior.

All of a sudden, the girl turned. Rehan's jaw dropped. He was stunned; his mouth was wide open, his body seemed tense and his hands became cold. He couldn't peel his eyes off her face—so familiar, yet lost in the past. He couldn't believe what he was seeing. Was all this a dream?

Time seemed to freeze. The hot vapor from the coffee cup rose slowly, people around him stopped speaking, the waiter's leg froze in mid-air and the butterfly on the table slowly moved its wings. As she walked towards them, Rehan's heart skipped a beat. The way she tucked her hair behind her ears gave him a sense of deja vu. Honey-colored eyes, rosy lips…the same smile. The closer she came, the deeper Rehan drowned in the ocean of his past. Their eyes met. It felt like two giant waves had just collided.

Anjali realized that her friend had reached their table, so she stopped speaking and turned. She held the girl's hand and smiled. "Remember him?" she asked.

The girl seemed to be speechless. She finally composed herself and uttered, "Rehan? Is it?"

"Yes, the one and only Rehan Mirza," Anjali said. "You know what, Rehan? I had not told her that we were going to meet you. So, she is kind of surprised to see you."

"Yeah…" Rehan said as he looked at Anjali.

"Do you know her?" Anjali asked him.

Rehan was at a loss for words at that moment. His lips trembled as he pretended to not remember her name, even though he very well knew who she was.

"Kavya," Anjali said.

The trembling stopped, as he remembered everything.

The name brought back a huge wave of memories, like a tsunami. The pages of the past, which he had locked away, long ago, in the darkest corner of his heart, came rushing in. He didn't know which page to hold on to. His body was in the café but his soul was standing in the middle of a forest, where each tree had a thousand leaves on it and each leaf was like a beautiful painting. They were the paintings of his life. All the laughter, smiles and moments. He was lost in the maze of time. The only thing he could utter that moment was "Kavya."

Who were they? What had happened in their past?

Chapter 2
The Love

*Indian Institute of Technology, Indore;
five years back*

The Indian Institutes of Technology (or IITs) are home to some of the brightest minds in the country. There are only 16 of them in the country, and they are considered premier institutions for higher education. Only a select few from among the several hundred thousands of applicants make their way to the IITs every year.

IIT Indore is located in Simrol, a lush, green village that is about 25 km away from Indore, The campus is spread over an area of 510 acres. Although established in recent years, it has quickly become the top choice for tech-savvy students, primarily due to the research facilities and computer science department. Students from this IIT made it to the internationally renowned ACM ICPC coding competition finals twice, which earned the college a good name. Year after year, students with the best ranks joined IIT Indore and brought even more laurels to their institution.

Rehan Mirza, computer science, batch of 2009. When he had first heard of IIT as a teenager, he always thought of scholars, students with brilliant IQ, knowledge and marks. Some of his friends used to say that if you were from IIT, you got laid right away because chicks dig IITians (in their opinion).

Rehan had met some great minds in there, people who were good in studies, who had great thirst for knowledge and were eager to innovate. Sadly, the not-so-true part was that chicks didn't dig them that much. *I mean, do they?* Even he didn't know the answer—but, as far as he had seen, things never went that way.

Academics were just one aspect of the engineering life. If anything, IITs were known for their cultural fests and activities. Students are given exposure to all kinds of extra-curricular activities. They formed clubs, which the institution provided funds for.

The students arranged cultural events round the year, with least interference from college authorities. Students in IITs were trained to become independent and different from others. Ironically, most of them ended up in the 9-to-5 job queue.

In that herd of chickens were some pigeons who liked to live their lives differently, doing what they liked, following their passions, breaking the chains of society and flying free. It felt wonderful to hear that, among the thousands of bookworms were a handful of souls who dipped their minds in creative ink.

Rehan was one of the creative minds—in fact, one of the best IIT Indore had to offer. He was everything but an academic. He was a photographer, designer and painter. He was in all the creative clubs in college and also led the photography and art clubs.

Rehan was pretty much an outlier among his peers and he got a lot of shit for it. He never really cared much about any of the crap that some of his classmates said about him. He was constantly bombarded with questions: "How will you get a job?," "Why don't you study?," "Is this the correct way to lead your life?" It takes a great deal of courage and guts to do something out of the box and he had it all. Whenever he felt low or demotivated, he had his close friends to cheer him up.

He was also well liked by his classmates. He had a friendly face and was always smiling. He had a smooth and charming voice. The fact that he was handsome helped as well. He was tall and fair, and had dark grey eyes that kept wandering, trying to find the right frame. His messy hair fell over his forehead.

He walked his own path, challenging the mainstream. He did what he wanted and believed in making his own rules.

He was quite popular among the girls; many tried to flirt with him but he was never interested in any of them. Every time a girl approached him, he decided to hold back and wait for the perfect one—but he never came across anyone who would fit in his weird, wonderful life.

Three years had passed since he had joined college. He was still in search of his dream girl. It is said that if you desire anything with all your heart and mind, the universe rearranges itself to grant your wish.

Then, one day, it finally happened.

Winter had just arrived. The sun was going down and cold winds blew in the evening. Rehan was sitting in his room. The place was rather messy. Clothes lay on the bean bag; things that were placed on the table had not been moved since the first day of college; there were unwashed dishes under the bed; empty wafer packets littered the floor.

The room had a weird smell to it. Believe it or not, living in such a messy room felt different but good.

Rehan was sitting on the bed, sorting out pictures on his laptop. He had to send some good pictures from last month's events to the literary club for their monthly magazine. There were thousands of pictures clicked by eight photographers. All of them were from Rehan's photography club. As he was leader of the club, all of them had to send their pictures to him. Eight people, eight folders—each folder containing hundreds of pictures.

He had been through five of the folders. Before he opened the sixth one, he lit up a cigarette. He was bored. He finished the smoke and went back to the pictures.

He opened the sixth folder, which contained pictures by a guy named Mayankh. Most of them were from the *dandiya* night, held during *Janmashtami*. All the pictures were of girls. "What a pervert Mayankh is!" Rehan thought to himself. Several pictures showed the same group of girls. He picked one or two and impatiently scrolled down.

All of a sudden, his eyes caught something but he had scrolled past that picture already. He slowly scrolled back and stopped at that picture. "Oh my!" He was amazed. The picture was one of the same group of girls dancing with *dandiya* sticks in their hands.

What had caught his attention was the sight of the girl in the center, as she spun around with her hands up in the air. She was wearing the traditional *dandiya* garb—a colorful mix of red and blue, with beautiful embroidery on it. As she moved, her *lehnga* swirled around in a frenzy of color. The small mirrors on her dress reflected light in every direction. Her smile was refreshing.

She looked very beautiful. Her smile had a strange charm to it. Her eyes reflected sheer joy, which would make a thousand souls happy. Her face resembled that of a goddess who bestows love and happiness upon the humankind. While Rehan was busy admiring her beauty, he got a call. It was Anjali.

Anjali was then the head of the literary club, so she had to manage all the online and print matters, including the college magazine.

"Hi," Rehan said.

"Hey," Anjali replied.

"What's up?"

"Did you get the pictures done? We need them by tonight. The magazine is ready, only the pictures need to be added."

"Yeah, yeah, I know. I'm on it. I'll finish it by dinner and mail it to you."

"Don't mail it to me. I've got a lot of editing work to do. I've asked one of the juniors to coordinate with you. Share it with her. She is looking after this. I've shared your number with her. She might give you a call later."

"Okay."

"Cool." She hung up.

Rehan continued to look through the pictures but it was hard for him to concentrate. His mind was still stuck on that girl and her beautiful face.

He scrolled through the pictures quickly so that he would get another glimpse of her in some other picture, but he didn't. He felt a bit disappointed. He went back to the picture and looked at her. He saved the photo in his drive and continued to sort through the remaining pictures.

He finished looking through the rest of the folders in fifteen minutes. While he was compiling the set, he heard his phone beep. It was a message from an unknown number: *Hi Rehan sir. Anjali ma'am asked me to coordinate with you for the pictures.*

Rehan wrote back: *Yeah. She mentioned.*

Oh! I forgot to introduce myself. I'm Kavya from first year.

Hi Kavya, I'm working on the pictures. I'll let you know once I'm done.

Okay sir.

Don't call me sir.

Sure.

After half an hour, when he was finally done, he messaged her: Hey. It's finished. Give me your mail id and I'll send them to you.

Moments later came the reply: Kavya.kapoor03@gmail.com

"Hmm... Kavya Kapoor. Nice name!" Rehan thought to himself as he typed in her email id. As he was about to send the mail, he casually scrolled his mouse over her email. He stopped and sat up.

"Oh my god! Whaaaaaaaaaaaattttt? Is she...?"

It was the picture of that girl—the one he couldn't take his eyes away from earlier. It was the same face, eyes and smile. A smile crept up on his face—the desert of his misfortune was now beset with rain, sent by the goddess of happiness.

He had already uploaded all the pictures and was about to send them when he hesitated. He sat back for a while. Then, he went to the picture with her in it and pulled up Photoshop. He blurred out all the others in the background, darkened the surroundings and highlighted only her face. That done, he stacked it with all the other pictures and sent her the email.

As soon as he sent the email, he was tormented by questions. "What if she doesn't like it? What if she feels that I'm flirting or making a move on her and stop talking to me? What if she likes it very much?" All these possibilities played in his mind. Still, he felt a strange sense of happiness. He couldn't stop smiling.

He lay down on his bed; he couldn't get her image out of his head. Her smile kept popping up in his mind. He looked at the fan, hummed a Hindi song and smiled. *Filmy, isn't it?*

Moments later, his phone beeped—it was Kavya. He felt butterflies in his stomach. *Thank you for the pictures,* the message read. His eye caught something else—her display picture was now the picture he had edited and sent.

"So, she liked it!" he thought. It felt like he had won an award. He did a little dance.

Nice dp, Rehan replied, as he chuckled to himself.

Thank you and thanks to you.

You're welcome.

I saw your work, the pictures you've taken and your retouching skills. You really are an artist.

On reading her words, he blushed.

Thanks for the kind words. I just do what I feel like. I don't know if it's good or bad, he replied modestly.

It's certainly better than the rest of the students. Always feels good to hear that at least somebody here is following his or her dream. Not everyone has the guts to do what you are doing.

Rehan sensed something deeper in her reply—a desire hidden in her words. Perhaps there were some dreams she used to cherish once but had later hidden them away somewhere. *So... What is it you wanted to do?* he asked.

How did you know? She sounded surprised.

It's just a sixth sense, if you will. While you were appreciating me, I felt that a dreamer inside you was composing the words.

Yeah...I have always wanted to be a writer.

Wow! Then how come you are in IIT?

Family, parents. Their dreams and expectations.

Ha-ha. Same here.

This struck a chord between them.

So what do you write? Stories, poems, articles? Rehan wanted to take the conversation ahead, and know more about her.

Stories.

Love stories?

Yes.

Nice. Send me some of your stories, I would love to read them.

Yeah. Sure. By the way, where are you from?

Rehan realized that even she didn't want to end the conversation.

Bhubaneswar, he replied quickly.

Oh, nice place. I've been there once. They call it the temple city, don't they?

Yes. Very much they do. You will find temples there every hundred or so meters. And you are from?

Chandigarh.

The cleanest city in India! Nice.

Yeah. It's a small city.

Are all girls from Chandigarh as fair as you? Rehan joked. They both shared a laugh.

That night, they chatted for almost three hours. Starting from each other's family to food choices they discussed everything. Rehan learned a lot about Kavya. She had an elder sister who lived in Delhi, and whom she loved very much. Her dad was a businessman, and was a very religious person. She told him about her mom and the delicious non-veg dishes she cooked. Kavya was a pure vegetarian; hearing about non-veg dishes made Rehan hungry.

Kavya's family had been living in Chandigarh since the 1970s. Her grandfather had started a business, and her father had continued it. She had done her schooling in Chandigarh. She proudly told him about all the medals she had won in writing competitions. She wanted to be a writer but her parents couldn't spot the aspiring writer under the skin of a scholar. Hence, she ended up in IIT.

Listening to her, Rehan looked back on his own life. His dad was a small bank's manager, who had always wanted his son to get into IIT—that was his only dream. Like Kavya's father, his dad also ignored the budding photographer in his school-topper son.

They talked about their favorite places, hobbies, movies, celebrities, songs, and a lot of other things. Kavya liked to travel but her parents didn't allow her to travel much, not even with her friends. They were over-protective of her. She was also an excellent guitarist, and used to play in her school events. She loved Shah Rukh Khan, and claimed to have watched all his movies at least ten times each. She was a movie buff.

By the time they reached the end of the conversation, they knew a lot about each other. They became friends, and good friends at that, in one night. No wonder, fate had a lot planned for them.

Before they said goodbye, Rehan asked her for a treat. Why? For the picture he had edited for her.

Before Kavya could say anything, he added, *At the canteen tomorrow morning. 6:30. Don't be late.*

Done. She replied.

And so their first official 'date' was fixed. As much as Rehan loved to sleep, the butterflies in his stomach didn't let him sleep that night; he kept picturing the date from various angles. He practiced some pick-up lines that he had found on the Internet. He even said them out loud in different tones to figure out the best way to say them. He also had a 'smile trial' in his bathroom, where he tried out different smiles in front of the mirror. He really wanted to make the best first impression, for she seemed to be the perfect girl for him. The girl he had been waiting for all these years.

The next morning, Rehan was found sleeping on his beanbag, with his long legs stretched out on the bed. He had dozed off after the all-night-long dialogue rehearsal he had had the previous night.

Somewhere in the distance, he could hear his phone ringing. After two or three rings, he felt it vibrate. It was on his crotch. He idly picked up the phone and looked at the time through sleepy eyes.

It was six-forty. "Oh my god!" he panicked. His eyes opened wide as he woke up instantly. He was supposed to be at the canteen by six-thirty to meet Kavya—and, now, he was late. Being late to your first date wasn't exactly the best impression.

While he was pulling himself out of the beanbag, he saw the phone again. Kavya was calling.

"Hello," Rehan said. His voice was stiff.

"Hi. I'm terribly sorry. I just woke up," she said, her voice sounding weary. Rehan wasn't paying attention to what she had said; his mind was lost in her melodious voice.

"It's okay." Rehan couldn't tell her that he had also gotten up just minutes before—that too, after hearing the phone. That would have spoiled his image. Instead, he added, "Come fast or you will have to drink cold tea."

His eyes were still struggling to stay open.

"I will be there in five," she said.

"Okay," said Rehan and cut the call.

He ran to the bathroom and splashed cold water on his face. He wiped his face, quickly put on some clean clothes and raced to the canteen.

It was a ten-minute-walk from his wing but he covered it in four-and-a-half minutes. He was panting heavily when he reached there. He went inside and sat at a table beside the window. He breathed slowly to make himself feel calm.

The canteen opened at six every morning, though people started coming from eight. So, it was empty when Rehan reached. He ordered a cup of tea. The canteen boy brought the tea and placed it on his table. Hot vapor, rising from the cup, appeared misty white against the light coming from the window. The view itself was very satisfying. Rehan was about to take a sip when he saw someone walking towards the canteen. It looked like a silhouette from a distance; as it came nearer, light washed away the shadow and it was clearer.

It was Kavya.

She was wearing a yellow t-shirt with 'I'm cute' written on it; black leggings displayed her feminine curves. She was taller than average; her hazel eyes sparkled behind her glasses. Her lips curved into a perfect smile. Her long hair fell around her shoulders.

As she walked towards him, he couldn't help but notice how beautiful she looked despite being in an *I-just-woke- up* outfit. He was so busy taking in her beauty that he forgot to gulp down the tea he had sipped.

Rehan smiled as she looked at him.

She remained standing there until Rehan told her to sit.

"Sorry," she replied, embarrassed.

"Ah, it's okay." He ordered tea for Kavya. "I drank your tea as it was getting cold," he joked. Kavya giggled.

"So, you aren't an early morning person," he remarked.

"No, I usually get up ten minutes before the class, brush my teeth and go."

"Ah…we used to do that, too."

"Used to?"

"Yeah. We don't go to college now. 'We' as in all the people from my group."

"Why?"

"Because we are in third year and college is boring. I don't have any interest in studying computer science at all. In fact, I hate coding. I prefer sleeping till noon, then waking up, having lunch and playing counter strike or FIFA with my friends then watching some movies before I go back to sleep. I feel better doing all those things than going to college," Rehan rambled before coming to a stop.

"Okay!" she laughed.

"How is the tea?" he asked.

"It's good."

"So, how are you liking the college?"

"Pretty well so far. College is good. Professors are nice. Subjects are fun. The hostel is good. I made new friends. Also joined two clubs."

"Which clubs?"

"Literary club and dance club."

"Dance?"

"My mom was a classical dancer. So it's in my genes. My elder sister is a professional dancer, too. She was the first runner-up in *Dance India Dance*."

"Riya Kapoor? Is she your sister?"

"Yeah."

"Wow! My mom watched that show. So, what does she do now?"

"She does shows with her team. She keeps travelling around."

"That's amazing."

"Yeah, it is. I always envy her. She did what she wanted to do. She followed her dreams. But I couldn't…"

"Why? What stopped you?"

She didn't say anything. She seemed uncomfortable and kept looking down.

Rehan comforted her and asked her the question again.

"My dad," she said.

"What? How?"

"When Riya auditioned for that dance show, she didn't tell dad. She knew he wouldn't allow this but she went there anyway. When he found out, he got mad. She won the entire nation's hearts but not dad's. When she came back to Chandigarh, the whole colony gathered to greet and congratulate her but dad didn't even talk to her. Mom and I thought he would get over it with time but he didn't. That incident scared me and I dropped the idea of writing."

"That's sad. Why is your dad like that?"

"He comes from a very conservative family where girls don't go showing up their body in skinny outfits and dancing in front of a camera for TV."

"That's nonsense."

She looked down again. Her face had lost its glow. She was probably feeling sad at that moment, so they remained quiet for some time. Perhaps she was reminded of her childhood.

Rehan felt bad for bringing up the topic in the first place. To cheer her up, he changed the topic. "So, did you have any interesting experiences in college yet?"

"No."

"Well, let me tell you one of mine."

And so he started talking about his first-year experiences.

"You know, Kavya, when I first came to this college, my roommate was a Bihari. I was so scared of him at first. He was a very quiet person…he did not talk or laugh. I was terrified of him. Then, one day, he walked out of the bathroom covered in soap. I couldn't control myself and I burst into laughter. Then I stopped, because he wasn't laughing at all. We looked at each other for a moment. His face was all serious. I thought I should apologize but he suddenly started laughing. I was stunned. He laughed his ass out. I joined him, too. We laughed so hard. Later, he turned out to be the coolest roommate I could ever have."

Kavya smiled. Her mood seemed to have become better.

Rehan talked about a few more things, such as how they had tossed a table from the fourth floor during their first year, how they had set fire to someone's pillow, and how they danced in front of the physics professor's house.

She laughed. He did save some of the best stories, though, for the future. They were chatting about her school days when she realized that she was getting late for college.

"I should leave now, otherwise I will miss the bus to college," she said.

Rehan didn't want her to go. He was so submerged in the conversation that it seemed a bit hard for him to come out of it.

"Yeah, okay," Rehan said in a neutral voice.

"I had a great morning. And thanks for the tea," she said as she got up.

"Ah. You are welcome."

"See you later," she said as she walked away.

Rehan looked at her as she walked away. Her hair bounced as she walked. She walked towards the door and, in the blink of an eye, she was gone, leaving behind a wonderful first-date memory for Rehan.

Rehan sat there for some time. Before going back to his room, he ran the whole conversation once more in his mind, and had two more cups of tea.

Back in his room, he couldn't stop smiling as he lay on the bed. He wanted to sleep badly, but the happiness within didn't let him. After some twisting and turning, he finally dozed off.

The next day, Rehan was in the garden, demonstrating the functions of a DSLR to the new members of his club, when he saw Kavya standing at a distance and looking at him. The garden was just in front of the girl's hostel, so she might have seen him.

Rehan called out to her to join him.

"Do you like cameras?" he asked Kavya.

"No. Not really, although I like to be photographed," she said with a naughty smile.

"Ha-ha. I bet you do."

He finished the demo and told the students to practice with the camera.

"Let's get some tea," Rehan said to Kavya.

She smiled and nodded. It was evening time and the canteen was full of people. Rehan found them a corner.

"So, how was your day?" he asked.

"It was good, although a weird thing happened today," she said.

"What?"

"Do you happen to know a guy named Vamsi?"

"Yeah. He's from our batch."

"Well, he was kind of hitting on me in the bus."

"Whaatttt? What did he do?"

"Urm…he sat next to me and was trying to force me to talk to him. I wasn't interested, I gave him a sign or two to show that but he didn't stop. I thought I could just pretend to hear him and it was going okay…until he put his hands on my thigh. It was awkward. He kept doing that throughout the way. When we reached, he asked for my number."

"Did you give it to him?"

"No."

"You did the right thing. But why didn't you say anything to him?"

"I was scared to make a scene. He was a senior."

"So what?"

"I don't know. I just couldn't."

"Don't worry. I'll take care of that son of a bitch."

"No! You won't do anything."

"I'll teach him a lesson that he will remember his entire life."

"No, please. I don't want any trouble."

"There will be no trouble. I assure you."

"How can you assure me of that if you are not around in college?"

"Well, in that case, I'll go to college."

"You will?"

"Yeah."

Kavya was both surprised and happy to hear that. She felt secure around him. His company had a positive vibe, which attracted her even more.

Later, she asked him about how he came across photography. Rehan narrated his journey from his school days. Kavya eagerly listened. Meanwhile, some people kept staring and pointing at them but neither of them cared.

Suddenly, Rehan asked Kavya out for a movie.

She was a bit surprised. "When?" she asked.

"Friday."

"But I have classes."

"We'll go for an evening show."

"Sounds good."

Rehan thought he had been quick in asking her out but since it turned out well, he didn't care much about it.

~Friday

"The movie was good," Kavya said, as she bit into the last slice of her pizza.

"Yeah. I liked it too." Rehan had already finished his and was sipping a cold drink.

It was getting late so they took a cab back to the campus. Rehan and Kavya sat in the backseat. The window was open an inch or so, and cold air brushed past their faces. The cab driver had put on a romantic song, probably one from a Shah Rukh Khan movie. Kavya was humming to the song. She closed her eyes and leaned against the window. Her left hand was on the seat, just an inch away from his thighs, her slender fingers tapping in sync with the song.

In that moment, she looked like an angel. Her eyes were closed, her hair was loose and waving around in the wind. Her face was illuminated by the red and yellow street lights.

He felt a sudden urge to take her hand into his and look into her eyes, but he couldn't gather the courage to do that. As he waited, he grew restless. His heart beat faster. He could feel every beat of the song, as if he was high. The tension seemed to grow with each passing moment.

He didn't know what made him do it, but the next thing he knew, his hand was on top of hers. He ran a thumb across her fingers and gave her hand a slight squeeze. A strange energy coursed through his body.

Kavya looked at him and smiled. This time, there was a hint of shyness. Rehan was worried that she would get angry but she didn't seem to mind. She closed her eyes again and didn't pull her hand away. He was relieved and didn't move his hand until they reached the campus.

Something sparked off between them that night. What was it? He didn't know—whatever it was, it felt beautiful.

~Two Weeks Later

Rehan was walking towards the college bus with a notebook in his hand—a very rare occurrence. On his way, he met some of his friends. They didn't look pleased on seeing Rehan going to college. They had a bewildered look on their faces. One of them even asked Rehan if there was an exam that day. Well, he wasn't entirely wrong. Since the first few weeks of the first semester, Rehan went to college only during exams.

"No. No exams today," he replied, laughing.

He climbed onto the bus and saw Kavya sitting alone. He walked over and sat beside her. As soon as he sat down, Kavya closed the diary she was writing in and kept it back in her bag.

"What was that?" Rehan asked.

"My journal."

Rehan nodded.

Just like in the canteen the other day, everybody stared at them. They just didn't care.

Rehan started going to college—not to attend classes but to spend more time with Kavya.

Kavya liked Rehan's changed habit. They would sit next to each other on the bus. He would wait for her to go to the canteen, and they'd eat together. Sometimes, she would wait for him to finish his lab, and head back to campus together. They enjoyed each other's company.

Time passed. Rehan and Kavya became closer.

~Few Months Later.

Fluxus.

If there was one thing IITs were known for, it was their famous cultural festivals.

Every year, IIT Indore held Fluxus, the annual cultural fest. Four days of party and fun. A window for chilling out all day long. The anti-nerd squad got the most benefits from it. Anyway, the nerds didn't add much value to the fest. It was all about the creative people who took part in it and made it grand.

It was the final event of the last day. KK was singing on stage and the whole crowd was singing with him too. Rehan and Kavya were in the front row. They held hands as they sang and swayed along with the crowd. The air was filled with energy and emotions as KK belted out one hit song after another. Rehan pulled Kavya closer and hugged her. He felt so close to her that he didn't want to leave her, ever. She hugged him back and they stayed like that for some time.

After an hour, the concert ended. Rehan and Kavya were heading back to the campus in a bus. The seats were mostly empty, as it was the last bus. They were sitting in the last row, in a corner. Rehan recalled the moment when Kavya was in his arms and smiled. He felt happy. He looked at her. She was smiling, too, and he knew they were thinking about the same thing.

As they looked at each other, the outside world seemed to fade away. Rehan leaned into her face as they came closer. She closed her eyes as his lips landed on hers. They felt soft and warm. They kissed long and hard.

He felt like grabbing her waist, laying her down on the seat and kissing her as much as he wanted, but he restrained himself. Neither of them wanted to let go but they had to when they became aware of the place and situation. Rehan held her close to his heart throughout the way. When they reached, he cupped her face with his palms before he moved away reluctantly.

They said their goodbyes and went to their hostels.

They weren't just friends anymore—Rehan knew that but did not convey his feelings to Kavya properly. Neither did Kavya.

This continued for eight months until the day finally arrived.

~Few Days after the Mid-Term Vacation

Rehan had been calling Kavya since morning, but she wasn't picking up. He even walked to the bus stop, hoping to see her, but he didn't find her there either. It annoyed Rehan. She had never behaved like this before. So he called her roommate, to find out if Kavya was okay or not. She said Kavya was fine, except that she was really upset about something ever since she had received a call from home. Rehan was worried now. He called her several times that day but she didn't pick up.

In the evening, Kavya called Rehan and asked him to meet her in the garden. Rehan was relieved that she had called. He quickly went to the garden. When he reached, he saw Kavya sitting alone on a bench. Rehan sat down beside her. "Why didn't you pick up my calls since morning? You know, I went searching for you in every bus. I looked like a fool."

"Sorry," she said in a low tone.

Rehan sat there silently, and looked at her. She looked miserable. Her eyes were sad and her face was pale. She had her hands wrapped around her legs. It was very unlikely of Kavya. He pushed her slightly with his shoulder to lighten the moment.

"What happened?" he said.

Kavya kept quiet.

Rehan asked again but she didn't say a word. Then, he put his arm around her shoulder and held her close and asked again softly. This time, there was so much love and concern in his voice that Kavya was moved to tears.

She finally spoke; "Dad called earlier in the morning. Riya is getting married."

"But that's good news!"

"Yes, it is. At first I thought he got over his anger after hearing about her marriage. But I was so wrong. He hasn't changed a bit. He warned me not to talk to Riya anymore." She stifled a cry. "When I called mom to find out what was going on, I found out that Riya is marrying a guy who is not from our caste and dad is furious about it. She said that he was ready to let go of the past and start afresh with Riya but this news has made him angrier."

"That's just nonsense. Who cares about all this in today's time?" Rehan tried to comfort her.

"I know, but he won't even let me and mom go to Riya's wedding."

She paused. Tears poured from her eyes. "I know Riya didn't call me because of dad. I love her, Rehan. I love her so much. She is my sister. How can I let her be alone on her wedding day?"

Rehan held her in his arms as she buried her face in his shoulder and cried.

They sat there for some time, watching the sun set in the distance. As it dipped below the horizon, Rehan led her to her hostel. He held her hand throughout the walk. When he dropped her at the hostel he told her not to worry, and added that everything would be alright.

Rehan walked back to his room. He couldn't stop thinking about Kavya's unhappy face. He was sitting on the bed, thinking about it, when he came up with an idea. He didn't know if it would work but he thought it was worth a try.

He opened his laptop.

~The Next Morning

Rehan was sleeping when he got a call from Kavya.

"Hi," she said.

"Hey. Morning," Rehan said in a sleepy voice.

"Listen, I'm sorry for yesterday," Kavya said. Her voice sounded low.

"It's okay. You don't have to be sorry."

"College?"

"Are you going?"

"Yes. nine-thirty bus."

"Okay. I gotto go freshen up then. I'll see you at the bus stop."

He had a smile on his face; he had a surprise for Kavya.

They were sitting in the bus, and Kavya was looking out of the window. She still looked harried from what had happened the previous night. Rehan thought this was the perfect time to surprise her.

"Hey, what are you doing the day after tomorrow?" Rehan asked her.

Kavya turned around. "Nothing. Why?"

"We're going somewhere."

"Where?"

"Kolkata."

"Kolkata? Are you mad?" Kavya said with a skeptical look on her face and looked away. Then, something struck her.

"Rehan?" she called him.

"Yeah."

"Why did you say we were going to Kolkata?"

"Actually, we aren't exactly going to Kolkata. There's this village named Taki, two hours from Kolkata. We are going there."

Kavya looked suspicious.

"Riya is getting married in that village," he added.

"What? How did you know that?" Kavya was all excited now.

"I pulled a trick!" Rehan smiled.

~The Previous Night

Rehan opened his laptop and searched for Riya's name on Facebook. He found her profile and sent her a message: Hi. This is Rehan, Kavya's friend. I want to talk to you about something. It's urgent.

The reply came just a few minutes later. Riya asked him if everything was alright. Rehan told her what had happened earlier in the evening. Riya said she knew Kavya would get hurt—that's why she had not called her, but she had no idea about her father's call.

Rehan offered to bring Kavya to the wedding. Riya refused at first but, when he reminded her about Kavya's tears, she couldn't refuse.

She thanked Rehan and said she would arrange for their transportation.

"You could've told me," Kavya said. There was a hint of surprise and happiness on her face.

"And what? Miss this expression on your face?" Rehan said as he laughed.

She playfully punched his arm.

~At the Airport

They were sitting in the lounge, waiting for the boarding call.

"I can't believe I'm going to Riya's wedding! It feels like a dream!" Kavya said.

"You are an SRK fan, right?" Rehan asked.

"Yes."

"Then you must have heard the dialogue from Om Shanti Om: *Kehte hein koi cheez ko agar poore dil se chaho toh poori kayinaat...*"

"*Usse tumse milane ki sajish mein lag jaati hai,*" Kavya completed the sentence.

They both laughed.

A few minutes later, the boarding announcement was made.

The flight duration was two hours; Rehan and Kavya slept throughout.

~Kolkata

"Excuse me, sir," Rehan heard someone calling his name and patting his shoulder. He opened his eyes. An air hostess was standing in front of him.

"Excuse me, sir, please straighten your seat. We are preparing to land."

"Sure," Rehan said and pressed the seat button. He saw that Kavya was asleep. She looked so relaxed that he didn't wake her up. The world outside the window appeared nearer as the plane descended. Before the wheels touched the ground, Rehan nudged Kavya so that she wouldn't wake up from the sudden impact.

As they walked out of the airport, Rehan saw a tall guy holding a board with both their names written on it. They walked over to him. He was wearing a white t-shirt and blue jeans. He had a good physique; his shoulder-length brown hair was parted to the left. He smiled as they approached him.

"You must be Kavya. You look just like your sister," the guy said. Kavya nodded. "And you must be Rehan," he said as he offered Rehan his hand.

"And you are?" Kavya asked.

"Aditya. Riya's fiancé."

"Oh!" Rehan and Kavya said simultaneously.

"Riya wanted me to pick you guys up."

"Why didn't she come?" Kavya asked.

"Uhm...she is busy with the preparations. There aren't many people at the wedding, so we pretty much arranged everything. But she is eagerly waiting for you. In fact, she has called me ten times since I reached the airport. She's gonna be very happy to see you."

They all sat in the car and left for Taki. Two hours later, they reached their destination.

As they entered Taki, Rehan was taken by surprise. It was not a typically poor village. It had proper houses, shops, electricity and, most importantly, good roads. This was not what Rehan had imagined.

Aditya stopped the car in front of a huge mansion that looked like an ancient palace. They got down from the car. Rehan looked at the tall brick structures while Kavya followed Aditya. She was getting restless.

Aditya walked into the house, with Kavya a few steps behind them, and Rehan following her. When they went inside, they saw Riya standing at the door to welcome her sister. Kavya was so happy that tears rolled down from her eyes. Rehan was very happy that he had brought Kavya to meet her sister. Riya thanked him and ushered Kavya inside for the *mehendi* ceremony. Rehan looked at her; Kavya looked happy and cheerful. He smiled and went to the guest room with Aditya.

Later in the afternoon, Rehan was resting on the bed when he heard a knock on his door. He opened the door, Kavya was standing outside. She was wearing a green *salwar* suit and had a big smile on her face. Her hair was left untied and fell over her shoulders. Her hands were beautifully lined with *mehendi*. Rehan invited her in.

"The *mehendi* looks beautiful," he said.

Kavya smiled and said, "Thank you for bringing me here. It means a lot to me."

Suddenly, Rehan realized how close they were standing. He could feel her warm breath on his neck. Kavya didn't make any attempt to move away. She gazed into his eyes and moved closer. Her hands brushed against Rehan's; she tiptoed as she placed a long sensuous kiss on his lips.

Time froze for a moment. Rehan was surprised. He saw her eyes—they were telling him something. He stood still for a second. He could still feel the gentleness of her lips. The heat of his body escalated with the rush of adrenaline. It seemed like both of them were standing at the edge of a cliff, and all they needed was a gentle push. And the push happened when Rehan grabbed her waist, pulled her closer and kissed her. They fell. Cleaving past the clouds, they fell into the infinity of love.

She put her hands around his neck and kissed him passionately. Bodies glued to each other, they fell on the bed. They squirmed around, feeling each other's bodies and kissing like there was no tomorrow. Through the window, the blue heaven witnessed them as they drowned in their love.

They lay on the bed, their bodies touching each other; the light started to fade as the sun began to set. Their faces were still visible in the dim light. He looked at her, as her face rested on his shoulders. There was pleasure in her eyes and a slight smile on her face. "Ah the joy of being together…" he thought to himself as he closed his eyes and snuggled closer to her.

Chapter 3

The Ice Breaker

18 January 2016

"Rehan…" Anjali said.

When her voice hit Rehan's ears, he became aware of his surroundings.

The sight of Kavya after all these years had pulled Rehan into a hurricane of memories. In a flash, he had relived the past all over again. Memories that he had buried deep within him had resurfaced again.

"Yeah," Rehan responded, as he took his eyes off Kavya.

She was still looking at him.

"Where were you lost?" Anjali asked.

"Nowhere," he shook his head. "I was just thinking about something. It's just…uh…it's not important. So, let's talk about your wedding destination." He still couldn't take his eyes off Kavya fully. One second, he looked at Anjali; the next, he peeked at Kavya.

"Rehan! I already told you a few minutes ago. You even nodded," Anjali said. She was surprised by his strange behavior.

"I'm sorry Anjali, I was a bit zoned out." Rehan was embarrassed. He felt sorry for not listening to his friend. Besides, it was not very professional of him. He looked apologetic.

"It's okay. Are you stressed about something? We can meet some other time if you want" Anjali suggested.

"No, no. It's alright. I was just thinking about something. And, like I said, nothing important." He focused all his attention on Anjali and tried to act as casual as possible.

"Okay then," Anjali said, and told him that they were having the wedding in Udaipur, Rajasthan. This time, Rehan listened to her intently.

Kavya sat there, looking at Rehan and Anjali. Though she didn't participate in the discussion, she nodded every time Anjali glanced at her, as if she were part of the conversation as well. However, she had something going on inside her mind. She was as shocked as Rehan, when they saw each other after a long time.

"Okay Rehan, I will send you the details of the location. We all are so excited to have you there," she said, and gave Rehan's arm a slight squeeze. She looked very happy. "See you at the wedding."

"Yeah, sure. I will be there a day before," Rehan said.

"Why?" Anjali asked.

"Sight inspection and all…you know, photographer's stuff."

Anjali smiled. "Okay then. See you there."

They all got up from their seats. Anjali shook hands with Rehan, and so did Kavya. After they left the café, Rehan remained seated, trying to compose himself, trying to believe the reality he was in.

"Hey, I think I forgot my phone inside," Kavya told Anjali after they walked out of the cafe.

"Okay. Go get it. I will be in the car," Anjali replied.

Kavya turned and hurried back to the cafe. As she stepped inside, she saw that Rehan was about to leave. She quickly walked over to him.

"Rehan…" Kavya called out.

He looked straight ahead; Kavya was standing in front of him. He was surprised to see her back again.

"I thought you had left," he said with a formal smile.

There was a moment of awkwardness as they looked at each other. Kavya tried to say something but the only thing she could manage was a mumble. It was obvious that she was nervous about something. She kept glancing out of the window, unable to meet his eyes.

Rehan stood there, waiting for Kavya to say something. He looked at her. "You…uh…wanted to say something?" he asked her gently, breaking the ice.

"No, I forgot my phone…just came to pick it up." Her phone rang at the exact same moment as she said that. It was inside her purse. She felt like an idiot. She pulled out the phone. It was Anjali.

"Got the phone. Coming in two minutes," she said quickly and ended the call.

She looked at Rehan. "Listen, I have something to tell you."

They both looked uncomfortable.

"Hmm…" Rehan nodded. He was drawing circles with his finger on the table next to him.

"Not here. Let's meet tomorrow. Someplace nice," she suggested.

"I don't know if I will be…" Rehan began but Kavya interrupted him: "Please. I have waited a long time to tell you this. Please!" Her eyes were begging for a 'yes' from Rehan, while his eyes were full of questions that he wanted answers for.

"Okay," Rehan said, a tad reluctantly. He didn't want to forgive her after all she had done to him but, for some reason, he wanted to listen to what she had to say.

"Give me your number. I will call you tomorrow," Kavya asked.

Rehan reached for his wallet and gave her his visiting card. He could have dictated his number but the uneasiness between them had thickened the barrier.

She thanked him and waved as she walked out of the cafe. She looked at the card and smiled.

She headed to the parking area where Anjali was waiting.

The things she had kept hidden inside were burning her up, yet the quick exchange with Rehan helped to brighten up her face. Finally, she would be able to explain herself. The burden she had been living with for the past five years was finally going to be lifted.

She reached the car.

"So what did he say?" Anjali asked Kavya.

"What did who say?" Kavya pretended to be unaware.

"Oh, come on! Don't act so innocent. Your phone was in your purse the whole time. You didn't take it out," Anjali said as she punctured Kavya's little lie.

Kavya felt sheepish. She tried to come up with an excuse but didn't have anything to say. So, she just looked out of the window, put her palm on her face and smiled.

"Looks like someone is going on a date this weekend," Anjali teased Kavya. They both laughed. Though Kavya joined in the laughter, she tried to avoid any more questions about Rehan. Anjali had to focus on driving, and, hence, didn't ask many questions as well.

They were on their way to Andheri, when they got stuck in heavy traffic. The cars barely moved an inch. Kavya was worried Anjali would ask her about Rehan again. So, she started talking about Anjali's wedding.

They were talking about the preparations and shopping, when Anjali suddenly said, "You and Rehan will look great together."

This was exactly what Kavya was trying to avoid—the name, that topic, the wave that would break all the barriers of her emotion and make them rush in.

"What gave you that idea?" Kavya said, pretending to hesitate.

"Did you know him in college?"

Anjali had been a nerd in college. *How do you think she got into Microsoft?* For four years, she didn't have a world outside her books. So, obviously, she was isolated from most of the gossip and happenings.

"Not really. I worked a few times with him but that was it."

"He was a popular student in college, though. Very funny and sweet guy back then. Don't know what happened to him in the last five years, he has become very silent and reserved." The traffic wasn't moving and the conversation was making Kavya uneasy.

"Turn the radio on. Let's see what songs are trending these days, so that we can play them at your wedding," she said to Anjali to change the topic.

Anjali blushed at the thought of her wedding. She nodded and turned on the radio. She switched to 93.5 RED FM.

"This song is dedicated to Sonam from Karthik. This is one of my favorite songs and I think many of us loved this song when it was released. A gem from the past. Let's hear it," the RJ announced.

Tum ho

Tum ho paas mere

Saath mere ho

Tum yun

Jitna mehsoos karoon tumko

Utna hi pa bhi loon

Tum ho mere liye

Mere liye ho tum yun

Khud ko mein haar gaya

Tum ko, tum ko mein jeeta hoon

Oooh ho...

ahmmm...

Aaah haa aa...

The song tore at Kavya's heart. She remembered Rehan playing the same song one beautiful evening. She couldn't help reminiscing about the past; her emotions flowed freely. It all felt like yesterday to her, although it had already been five years back.

She looked up at the sky through her window, hope filling her heart. Maybe, this time, it would work out alright.

Chapter 4
The Unexpected

Flashback

Khud ko mein haar gaya

Tum ko, tum ko mein jeeta hoon

Oooh ho...

ahmmm...

Aaah haa aa...

Kavya closed her eyes, feeling every beat of the song. Her fingers were intertwined with those of Rehan's. Their bodies, bare and warm, lay tangled beneath the blanket. Her toes drew circles on Rehan's shin. He smiled at her. The love bugs had done their work.

Rehan brushed his fingers through her hair, cupped her face and kissed her. A wide smile appeared on her lips. She opened her eyes and saw Rehan looking at her. She felt complete in that moment.

She snuggled closer to Rehan, and rested her head on his chest. A while back, they were two bodies and two souls; now, they were one.

They were so lost in each other that they lost track of time. They were floating in their own paradise of love. Suddenly, Kavya heard Riya calling out to her.

Kavya got up, holding the blanket close to her chest.

"I gotto go," she said and jumped off the bed with the blanket.

"What the hell? Give me the bedsheet. It's too cold!" Rehan said, putting the pillow over his crotch.

"Ha-ha. No. Get up and put on your clothes," Kavya said with a sly grin and walked into the bathroom with her clothes.

She came out while Rehan was putting on his underwear. She laughed.

"Okay, I'll go and help Riya. You get some rest," Kavya said as she went closer, stood on her toes and stole a kiss. They both smiled.

"Don't you need rest, too?" Rehan asked jokingly.

"Yes."

"Then come, rest. No?" he said, pointing to the empty side of the bed.

"Nice try," she said as she slowly opened the door, peeked through the thin gap and walked out. She couldn't stop blushing. A warm glow spread through her entire body. Though she was out of the room, her soul resided inside it with Rehan.

~Later that Evening

Kavya was downstairs. All the ladies were sitting around, getting *mehendi* drawn on their hands. Kavya also helped draw the *mehendi*. She was not a professional but she was pretty good at it. The beautiful spiral patterns and intricate designs looked like works of art, and the smell of henna hung in the air.

The elderly women sat there talking to each other. Somehow, the topic about Riya and Kavya's facial similarities came up. Some of them admired Kavya's soft features while others took Riya's side.

Kavya didn't take anything seriously. She knew that her sister was more beautiful. She only thought about Rehan. A naughty smile crept across her face as she remembered Rehan's expression when she snatched the bedsheet from him. Apparently, she wasn't very good at hiding her emotions. She kept giggling.

"Who's that handsome boy with you? Is he your boyfriend?" one of the ladies asked, bringing Kavya back to reality.

She blushed. "Ha-ha, no. We are just friends," she said.

"Hmm.... Just friends!" the lady said in a teasing tone. They all laughed.

Kavya was busy drawing *mehendi* when an old lady came up from behind with a wooden box. "Kavya, take this sari and *kangan* to your sister. She will wear them tomorrow," she instructed her and handed over the box.

Kavya looked at the box. It was made out of mahogany and the grain gave it an interesting texture. It looked old but it was beautiful. Tiny elephant and horse figures were carved on its side, with a fine floral design on top.

"Only family members can give this to the bride—it is our family tradition. Since you are the only family she has here, you should give it to her," said another elderly lady from the group.

"Okay," said Kavya, as she took the box and walked up the stairs to Riya's room.

She was unfamiliar with such traditions, because all the weddings she had been to until then had been mainstream Punjabi-style weddings. So, this ritual seemed strange to her.

Riya's room was on the far left side of the *haveli*, where no one could hear anything from the hall outside. Overhead lights illuminated the red carpet, and tapestries lined the hallway.

As she went closer to Riya's room, she heard someone sobbing. She looked through the partially open door. Riya was sitting in front of the mirror, crying. She seemed to be talking to someone. A grumpy voice came from the other end. Moments later, Kavya realized it was her dad.

"Dad…how could you say this to me?" Riya said, her voice broken.

A chill ran through Kavya's spine.

"How dare you marry a guy out of our caste?" Her dad's voice was loud and angry.

Kavya felt her heart sink.

"If you won't come, at least let mom come to the wedding, please," Riya was still pleading.

"Don't you dare call us again! We have no relationship with you anymore," her dad said.

His rude voice pierced Kavya's heart. She always thought that, even though her dad was angry with

Riya, everything would be fine in a few months. She was wrong.

On hearing her father talk like that, she was stunned. Which daughter could hear such things from her father? Tears rolled down from both their eyes. Kavya held the box against her chest and tried not to break down. She couldn't let her sister cry. She wanted to go inside and hold her tight in her arms, and comfort her, but she couldn't gather the courage to do so. Riya had already cried her eyes out, and Kavya didn't want to add any more tears to it.

She stood there for a while, after her dad ended the call. Then, she heard Riya sobbing and walking towards the door. She quickly got up and pretended to walk towards the room, and wiped away her tears.

Riya came to the door, and almost bumped into Kavya.

"I was just coming to hand you this," Kavya said, pointing to the ornate wooden box.

"Put it on the table over there." Riya motioned to her to come in.

Kavya put the box on the table. She could see tear marks on Riya's face but she didn't say anything. Riya faked a smile and asked her if she liked Aditya's folks.

"They are good people," Kavya said.

"Where's Rehan? Is he still sleeping? Tell him to have dinner otherwise he will have to sleep empty stomach. These people eat very early," Riya said. She avoided looking at Kavya.

"Yeah, I will tell him. Uh…are you ok? You look a bit pale," Kavya asked.

"Ha-ha. Sweetheart, I got this. It's just the wedding pressure. But you came here, and that's more than enough for me. Now, go and take care of your friend."

"Are you sure you don't need anything?"

"Yeah, baby. You go take care of Rehan. I will call you if I need anything."

"Okay. I will go and wake him up."

"Hmmm. And you also have dinner."

"Okay." Kavya said as she walked out. She felt bad for her sister, but she knew how strong Riya was. She would handle it the same way she had handled everything till now. She was more independent than any other person Kavya had known in her life. Further, being her older sister, Riya had always been Kavya's main confidante. That's why she had always loved and admired Riya.

Kavya was walking down the hall when a thought crossed her mind. All of a sudden, she felt queasy and her legs felt wobbly. She quickly went to her room, closed the door and sat down on the sofa.

Over the past few months, she had been so happy with Rehan that she had never thought about their future. Although she had known this subconsciously, the fun had always overshadowed it.

Now that she heard her dad talking, her dreams of a life with Rehan came crashing down.

"This is never going to work," her reflection seemed to say as she looked at the mirror.

"What?" she asked.

"You, Rehan. All of this," the reflection replied.

"Why?"

"Don't be naive. You know very well."

"But this is different. I am sure dad will understand." Even she could hear the doubt in her voice.

"You think? Your dad just ended the relationship with your sister because she married a guy out of their caste. And you, sweetheart, are going for a guy who is out of your religion."

"B…But I love him."

"But are you as strong as your sister? Do you think you can bear those cruel words from your father? You are too weak, Kavya, and you can't afford to lose your parents. You are going to destroy both your lives. You know the path you are taking has a dead end ahead."

"I can't leave him. He cares for me. He loves me."

"And do you?"

"Do I what?"

"Do you care for him?"

"Of course I do."

"Then leave him as he is. Don't make him dream of a life with you, which you can't promise. It will break his heart."

"I can't leave him."

"You have to. You have two choices. Either go with Rehan and lose your parents forever, like your sister did, or lose him. Which one do you think is easier? He is a good guy. He will find someone better than you and you will find someone, too, eventually. But once you lose your parents, you lose them forever. It's not too late. Stop the ship when it's still near the harbor or sail into the storm and destroy everything you have."

Kavya pressed her knees closer to her chest and lay down on the sofa. Everything the reflection told her was true. She was too weak to fight her parents and she loved Rehan too much to see him suffer heartbreak. Her mind was in turmoil.

Finally, she made her decision and wrote it down in her journal. It took all her strength not to break down into tears while she was jotting it down.

She kept staring at the mirror until she finally fell asleep.

~Next Morning

Kavya slept on the couch the whole night. At six in the morning, she heard her phone ring. Riya was calling.

"Hello." Kavya's voice was sleepy.

"Morning sweetheart," Riya greeted her.

"Morning di. What happened?"

"Nothing baby. Whenever you get up, just come and meet me. I need a little help."

"Hmm. Okay di," said Kavya, as she hung up the phone. She saw Rehan's missed calls. Her instant reflex was to call him but she stopped. She put down the phone and closed her eyes. She opened them a moment later and looked at the mirror. She saw the reflection; it was smiling at her, as if to say, "You are doing the right thing, honey." She closed her eyes and went back to sleep.

It was nine in the morning and preparations were in full swing. The *mandap* was being set up. The gigantic, colorful canopy in the middle of the quadrangle looked magnificent. Colorful flowers lined the *mandap*.

The men were enjoying the view and gossiping while the ladies were busy setting things up. People were walking from here and there, carrying things or shouting orders. The weather was pleasant and a bit cloudy.

Everyone could feel the excitement in the air.

Slowly, the guests started coming in. Most of them were from Aditya's side but some of Riya's colleagues were also present. The photographers were busy taking pictures and setting up their equipment. Although there weren't a lot of people, it looked like a grand wedding.

Unlike most Bengalis, Aditya's family held the wedding during daytime. It was a tradition that their ancestors had followed for quite some time. Everyone in their family got married in the morning, in order to avoid some kind of *kula-dosha* (fault in the family line).

After everybody settled down, the wedding rituals began.

Kavya and a few of the other girls brought Riya downstairs. Kavya walked her down the aisle to the *mandap*, where Aditya was sitting.

Riya wore a red sari and looked very beautiful. She was covered in jewelry from head to toe. Everybody had their eyes on her.

Kavya had worn an orange suit with pink borders. It was a simple outfit but she looked very elegant.

Kavya was standing by Riya's side when she saw Rehan coming down the stairs. He wore a blue *kurta* over a white pajama and he looked fresh and handsome. For a moment, she forgot about her decision. She couldn't keep her eyes off him. Riya noticed this and nudged her. "*Dhyan kahan hai tera?*" she said.

"*Kahin nahi,*" Kavya said as she stopped staring and looked straight ahead.

Riya sat down beside Aditya while Kavya stood close to her. Although she could see Rehan, she was determined not to meet his eye.

Rehan, on the other hand, had no one else to talk to. He tried many times to get Kavya's attention but nothing worked. Kavya strengthened herself;

she knew she had to do this. One after another, the wedding rituals took place and Kavya got so busy in helping out her sister that she forgot about Rehan.

Later she saw Rehan talking to the girl who was taking photographs. They were laughing and having a good time. She felt a pang of jealousy. She felt like getting up, walking to Rehan and dragging him to her side. But she stood there, by her sister's side.

During the *feras* (when the bride and groom walk around the fire), it started raining. The canopy on the mandap was covered with plastic sheets, so the rituals didn't stop. People found shelter in the nearby canopies but Kavya stood there, getting drenched in the rain. Riya told her to come inside but she didn't. She stood there. She wanted the rain to wash away her tears, and the roaring thunder to swallow her pain. The cold droplets felt like tiny prickles on her skin. It was comforting in a way. She closed her eyes for a bit and tuned out the outside world.

Rehan was standing under a small canopy a few meters away. He called Kavya to come there and take shelter but she didn't respond. When Kavya didn't listen to him, he ran over and stood beside her. He put both his palms over her head to try and protect her from the rain. Suddenly, Kavya felt fewer droplets falling on her. She opened her eyes and there was Rehan, standing by her side, shielding her from the rain. She had never felt so cared for in her life. She wanted to hug him and feel sheltered inside his warm arms, but she gulped down her feelings and didn't react. She stood there, still and expressionless.

Rehan didn't understand her unusual behavior. He thought she might be sad knowing that her sister would not be present in her life anymore. He also wanted to shower his love on Kavya and comfort her. They were both drenched; raindrops crawled down their faces, touched their lips and fell from their chins. Then, Rehan spotted the tears in her eyes. He put his hand on her shoulder and held her tightly. She felt Rehan's hand on her shoulder but she stayed calm. She didn't react and did not look at him either. By the time the *pandit* finished his chanting, the rain had stopped. The couple took the *pandit's* blessings.

After that, Riya walked down the *mandap*. Kavya walked over to Riya, escaping Rehan's arms. Rehan felt put off as Kavya didn't look at him even once.

~The Next Day

Kavya and Rehan had to head back to college—to their normal life, which was not so normal anymore.

Kavya packed her stuff and directly went downstairs. She didn't call Rehan because she didn't want to face him. Rehan came shortly after. He was surprised that Kavya hadn't woken him up or called him downstairs. He came and stood beside Kavya. They looked at each other. Her eyes didn't have the warm, friendly look they usually did. Rehan didn't understand; he was about to ask her when Riya and Aditya came in.

"So you guys are ready to head back?" Riya asked. She looked at Rehan.

"Yes," Rehan replied. Kavya also nodded.

"Thank you, Rehan. If it hadn't have been for you, I would have missed Kavya so much," Riya said.

"Yes. She is right. And you are lucky to have a friend like him, Kavya," Aditya joined in.

Kavya nodded silently.

"Aditya and I will drive you to the airport," Riya said.

"No. There's no need, di. We will take the bus," Kavya said, as she didn't want to sit alongside Rehan again.

"With the busy schedules and all, we didn't have a good chat since you guys have arrived. So, we will talk on the way to the airport," Aditya suggested. Riya agreed.

"Okay. Sounds cool," said Rehan.

They all headed to the car. Riya sat in the front seat beside Aditya, and Kavya sat with Rehan in the rear seat. On the way, Aditya asked Kavya and Rehan about how they had become friends, life in college, the funny things they did in college and loads of other questions. Kavya didn't speak much. She added a few words here and there, while Rehan answered Aditya. Riya also joined in; she asked Rehan about his family and his future plans. To Rehan's surprise, Kavya, who used to admire and appreciate his passion for photography, didn't say a word. She remained quiet while Rehan carried on the conversation with Riya and Aditya.

After two hours, they reached the airport. Time had passed by very fast amidst their conversations. Riya hugged Kavya, and wished her well. She added that she would meet her if she got a chance to visit Indore. Kavya was happy to hear that. Before saying goodbye, Riya asked Kavya if anything was troubling her. Kavya lied to her and said everything was okay. She said she tense about the upcoming exams.

Kavya and Rehan walked into the airport, and waved goodbye to Riya and Aditya.

Inside the airport, Kavya walked straight to the check-in counter. Rehan followed her. He wanted to talk to her but he thought it would be better if he gave her some space; he thought she was missing her sister. Yet, he couldn't shake off the feeling that she was bothered by something else.

Kavya was quiet on the flight as well. When Rehan asked about it, she pretended to have a headache and slept the whole time. She didn't talk to him. She was waiting to reach college where she wouldn't have to be with Rehan, and it would be easier for her to end things.

They reached the campus. Kavya walked fast, as if she were in a hurry. When they reached the girls' hostel Kavya walked straight into the building even as Rehan tried to say something. She didn't stop or turn around. Rehan stood there for a while after Kavya disappeared, and then walked to his room, feeling dejected.

The next few days, Rehan tried calling her but she didn't pick up her phone. She didn't reply to his texts. This caused him to become anxious. So, he waited near the hostel for her to come down but she didn't. He even waited at the college bus stop to meet her but she didn't go to college. He realized that she was trying to avoid him. He started getting desperate. He kept calling her all day. When all his efforts seemed to be in vain, he tried calling Gurpreet, her roommate. She didn't pick up the call either. One by one, the cards were starting to fall.

Over the next few days, they had their end-terms. Their exams were held in the morning.

On exam day, Rehan walked to the bus a few minutes earlier, hoping to find Kavya, but she had already taken another bus. The same thing happened at college. This troubled Rehan. He couldn't study or do well in the exam because he was so frustrated. One after another, all his exams were horribly bad experiences. Yet, he kept going to college—so that he could meet Kavya once at least. He was like the warrior who went to war despite consecutive defeat, in the hope that he would win one day.

It was the last day of exams. The end-term break would start the next day and everyone would be going home. As soon as the exam ended, Rehan wanted to talk to Kavya. It would be his last chance to talk to her before she flew home. So, he finished his exam an hour earlier, took a taxi to the campus and waited for Kavya at the girls' hostel. He knew he would see her today, and he was praying that nothing bad should happen. He was tense. He hadn't slept properly for days. He had lost patience. He kept praying until he reached the campus.

An hour later, Kavya came.

She was walking with her friends towards the hostel when Rehan saw her. He walked towards her. Kavya was busy talking to her friends and she didn't notice Rehan approaching her. He barged into the group, grabbed her hand and told her to come with him as he pulled her out. Kavya was too shocked to do anything; she followed him.

He took her into the garden, to the same place where Kavya had cried the other night. He turned around and looked at her.

Kavya was scared of Rehan after his sudden outbreak. She stood there quietly, holding her bag tight. She couldn't meet his eyes.

"What's going on?" Rehan asked Kavya. His tone showed the anger that was raging inside him.

"Nothing." She was still not looking at him.

"Really? I am not a fool, Kavya." Rehan raised his eyebrows in anger. "Why are you avoiding me?"

"What? What are you talking about?" This time, she looked into his eyes. They were red.

"I think you know."

"No, I don't. Please tell me."

"Let it be if you don't remember."

Perhaps he was being too harsh. He lowered his voice and said, "But why aren't you taking my calls or replying to my messages? Did something happen? Is it about the thing we did that day? Is that making it weird for you to talk to me?"

"No..." She paused and acted as if she was irritated. She continued, "I have forgotten about it already. We both know it was a weak moment and we both fell for it. It's not a big deal. And about not receiving calls, I was busy preparing for my terms, so I was avoiding using the phone." She sounded casual but she was burning with grief inside. It took all of her strength to lie about that day. She remembered each moment they had spent together over the previous few days. All she wanted to do was hug him and tell him everything was alright, but she held herself back. She couldn't believe she was saying all this to Rehan—the person she valued more than anyone else.

"What? No big deal? Exams? What are you talking about, Kavya? I don't think you are telling me the truth. Please tell me. Did I do something wrong?" Rehan pleaded as he grabbed her hand tightly.

Kavya had never wished to see this side of Rehan, and she hated herself when she realized that she was reason behind his transformation.

"What's the matter with you Rehan? Why are you acting like a psycho?" Kavya asked, genuinely irritated now, but her irritation was centered on her own behavior. She tried to wrestle her hand from his grip.

Rehan was perplexed by the sudden change in her behavior. Kavya seemed to be a different girl altogether. He couldn't understand why she was doing this. It took him by surprise that the girl who used to hold his hand was now pulling away her hand away from him. He couldn't understand why the girl who used to admire him was calling him a 'psycho' now. Was he in some alternate reality, where Kavya had never loved Rehan?

"What's happened to you?" Rehan asked.

"Nothing. I'm the same as I was."

"Then why are you behaving like this?"

"Then how do you want me to behave?"

"Be the girl you used to be…"

"I'm the same girl."

"No, you are not."

"Don't talk nonsense. You are giving me a headache," she said. Her tone was cold. She was putting on a great show; the real Kavya had taken a backseat inside of her. It felt like she had turned into a paralyzed human who could see and hear but couldn't do anything about what was happening around her.

At the other end of the conversation, after being shot by crude and cold arrows, Rehan had become numb. He didn't want to argue further and hear something unexpected from the girl he loved the most. So, he took up the final question—the most important one of all.

"Okay, I will ask you one last thing. Answer me and I will let you go," Rehan said. He calmed himself down and lightened his grip on Kavya's hand.

"Okay. Ask." Kavya felt a bit relieved; the conversation was probably coming to an end.

"Do you love me?" he asked. He stood still and waited for her answer, his eyes welling up with tears.

"No."

As she said that word, it felt like a thousand spears had pierced her heart; unbearable pain broke out inside her, but she didn't let her emotions show on her face.

Rehan's hand went slack. His eyes lost their glow, and his lips quivered. He kneeled down on the ground. The 'No' from Kavya echoed in his ears. He wanted to yell and argue with her but his voice was choked. All those happy evenings, those moments spent with each other came crashing down on him. Even the wintry wind seemed to mourn his fate.

Kavya broke down inside. She had never thought she would see Rehan like this. She turned around and left him, still kneeling in the grass.

She wanted to go back to Rehan and tell him that she loved him. She wanted to say that she was afraid of her parents, and that this was all a lie. She wanted to kiss him and hug him tightly. But she couldn't. The moment had passed. She couldn't take it back.

So, she walked back to her hostel. She burst into tears as soon as she entered the lift. No one saw her. She cried like she had never cried before.

Both of them cried a river. Nobody could tell who was hurt more but, from Rehan's point of view, he had lost everything.

He was in the garden, on his knees, mourning fate's cruel joke on him.

Chapter 5
The Alcohol

18 January 2016

It was three in the afternoon. Rehan was driving back home.

He looked out his window. The sky was a bit overcast. Winter never had much of an effect on Mumbai. The roads were also relatively empty at this hour, so the drive wasn't much of a headache.

The meeting at the café was still fresh in his mind. Try as he might, his mind drifted back to Kavya. He was all messed up. After everything that had happened five years ago in college, meeting Kavya was the last thing he wanted. The wounds that had taken so long to heal were torn open again. It had taken a good portion of the last five years to get over her, but fate seemed to have a cruel sense of humor.

Rehan reached his apartment. He slumped down on his bed, wishing the warm mattress would swallow him up. His mind went back to the meeting with Kavya. Why did she want to meet him after all this years? Was it not enough that she had destroyed his life five years ago?

Memories flooded his mind. The days they had spent together, sharing each other's lives and having so much fun.

"No, Stop. You've already hurt yourself enough. No need to dwell on the past," he said to himself.

He pressed the pillow against his head in an effort to block out the thoughts but to no avail. Frustrated, he got up and put on some music to drown his thoughts. As he increased the volume, the intensity of his thoughts also increased. The music was so loud that the alarm clock on the mantle began to vibrate.

It was like a wound—the more he scratched, the more it itched.

Meanwhile, Tulika called. He felt a bit relieved and picked up the call.

"Hey!" Tulika's voice was cheery as always.

"Hi," Rehan replied unenthusiastically.

"Are you alright? You sound a bit low."

"It's nothing. Just a headache."

"Okay. So, how did the meeting go?"

"Yeah it was alright. The usual stuff, you know."

"Good. *Acha* listen, I am flying to Udaipur for a project."

"When?" Rehan was a bit surprised.

"Tomorrow morning."

"Why didn't you tell me before?"

"It was all so sudden. Actually the stylist for the photo-shoot backed out at the last moment, so they are sending me there."

"Oh."

"Don't worry, I will be back in a day or two."

"Wait. Wait. Wait. You are coming home today, right?" He had been waiting for Tulika to come back home so that he could discuss the today's events with her. She was the only one he was close to.

"Uh…actually no. I have to prepare for tomorrow so I will be staying over at the office and will catch the morning flight. Sorry."

"It's alright." Rehan paused. "I will miss you."

"Awww…me too. Don't worry, I'll be back by Saturday. And I might have a surprise for you."

"Surprise?"

"Yep."

"What surprise?"

"It's called a 'surprise' for a reason, Rehan." He could imagine her rolling her eyes on the other end of the phone. It made him chuckle.

"I gotto go now. Take care," she said as she hung up.

Rehan threw the phone on the bed and lay down again. Talking to Tulika made him feel better but he was still thinking about Kavya. He closed his eyes but he was too restless to sleep.

All of a sudden, he got up and walked to Tulika's room. He went to the bottom closet and opened it. He saw bottles lined up in an orderly fashion. Tulika was an alcohol connoisseur; there were exquisite wines and whisky—some of them branded and expensive, others just cheap stuff to get drunk on. They used to spend countless hours tasting and enjoying the various drinks.

Tonight, Rehan was looking to get drunk. He picked up a bottle of whisky and went back to his room. He poured out a drink and gulped it down in one go. He felt a burning sensation as the whisky washed down his throat. He drank almost half the bottle, wishing to drown his misery in alcohol. His eyes became red and bleary. Sweat lined his forehead.

He took off his shirt and tossed it aside. The sun was about to set, and its rays lent an orange hue to the room. His body looked like that of a sculpture, with every bulge and curve of his muscles accentuated by the soft light filtering through the window.

It was funny, Rehan thought, as he looked at the bottle of whisky. Being with Kavya had been like tasting alcohol—the first time you had it, you liked it. And before you knew it, you were too addicted to let go. Drowning in the sweet relief that it provided from this miserable life. When you finally decided to stop, to let go, you just couldn't do it. Slowly, you realized that the world was not as comfortable as it seemed, that it was all an illusion and reality came crashing down on you.

The moments he had spent with Kavya were some of the best of his life. Now that he wanted to leave them behind, they haunted his soul and made him miserable.

He lit up a cigarette and watched the sun going down the horizon. As the last of the rays faded away, he lay back and looked at the ceiling. The room seemed to spin around him and his vision became blurry. He closed his eyes but time seemed to have slowed down. Sometime later, he drifted off to sleep.

Chapter 6

The Change

Flashback

Rehan was still in the garden, mourning his break-up with Kavya. He felt defeated and lost. Tears rolled down his face. He still couldn't believe that Kavya had broken up with him. Never in a million years would he have imagined that she would do this to him. After all the time they had spent together, he thought there was something between them, something that kept them with each other.

Had he imagined all that? He wasn't the only one who had enjoyed all those moments—they had both been happy together. What went wrong?

His mind harbored a hurricane of emotions. Color seemed to drain out of his life. He sat there, crying.

After a while, he heard people approaching the garden. He pulled himself together and got up, and wiped the tears on his sleeves. He didn't want to be seen teary-eyed in front of his classmates, so he cloaked his misery with a smile and started walking.

He walked to his room. On the way, he met a few of his friends on the other side of the road. They called after him but he didn't pay heed. The pain of heartbreak seemed to have disabled his senses temporarily.

When he reached his room and opened the door, he saw that all his roommates were celebrating as the exams were over. Everyone was drinking. When Rehan entered, one of his roommates handed him a beer.

"It's Goa time, bitch!" he said, and everyone screamed, "Yay!"

Rehan didn't react. He put the bottle back on the table and went straight to his room. He slammed the door behind him and sat on the bed. His legs were no longer able to carry his weight. He sat there, staring at the wall. A moment later, tears welled up in his eyes.

He took out his phone and looked at the pictures of Kavya and him. There were hundreds of them. They looked so happy in those pictures. He kept swiping them, one after another; he couldn't stop until he saw the very first picture of them together. It was from the first time they had gone on a date.

Kavya was trying to bite a slice of the pizza when Rehan took a picture of her secretly. She saw Rehan taking the picture so she covered her face with her hand.

All those pictures reminded Rehan of how close they had been with each other, how much they enjoyed all those beautiful moments together. He relived each and every moment in those pictures. The more he looked at the picture, the more pain he felt—the pain of not being with her again. He put the phone aside and lay down on the bed. He cried his heart out. Some time later, when his eyes were dry, he passed out. Though he was asleep, he was still sobbing.

He slept through the evening and night.

He woke up at nine the next morning. His hair was messy, face was swollen and his eyes were struggling to stay open. As soon as he broke out of the dizziness, he looked around for his phone, it was on the bed. He grabbed it and called Kavya. He hurriedly dialed her number.

He wanted to talk about what had happened the previous day. He wanted to make things right. He wanted to remind her of all those happy moments they shared, all those things they talked about, and all those hours they texted each other. He was ready to give her whatever it took to patch things up. He was ready to fight again. But she didn't pick up the call. He called her many times but not once did she answer. He texted her. One after another, he wrote several texts but nothing came back in return.

He was getting desperate and restless. He got up and ran to the girl's hostel.

As soon as he reached, he walked straight into the reception. The lady guard, who was sitting there, looked at Rehan. She stopped him, as boys were not allowed to enter. She had seen him many times with Kavya, so she talked to him. Rehan asked her about Kavya. She said Kavya left for her home that morning itself and that she would come after the holidays.

Rehan stood there, clueless. He didn't know what to do.

Helpless, he went back to his room. He had never felt this lost before. He hadn't eaten anything since the previous day. He was feeling dizzy, and his skin was pale and dry.

He lay down on the bed and tried calling Kavya again. This time, his calls didn't even go through. He called her a couple more times but it didn't work. He was surprised; it seemed very odd because he had called her just a few minutes back. "May be some network issue," he said to himself. He got up, went to the other room, borrowed his roommate's phone and dialed her number. The call went through. A few rings later, Kavya picked up the call. Her voice rang in his ears like a sweet symphony. As soon as Rehan started talking, she hung up. He didn't understand. He now called her from his phone. The call didn't go through. "What's happening?" he thought. To make sure that everything was okay with his phone, he dialed his friend's number—the phone in his other hand started ringing. He realized that Kavya had blocked his number. This made him desperate. He ran from one friend to another to borrow their phones and call her, to hear her voice once again. He dialed her number so many times that he didn't have to look at the phone now. He could effortlessly move his fingers and dial her number. Like a mad man, he tried every possible way to reach her. When he got tired of watching all his efforts turn to waste, he gave up. He understood that he had lost the battle. His shoulders sagged with disappointment.

He sat there for a while. He could feel the cracks in his heart. Piece by piece, it started to break, while he sat there, staring at the wall. Memories kept flashing through his eyes, and gave rise to tears. He was still holding the phone. He didn't move at all. He sat there like a statue. Then, all of a sudden, he got up; his face was flushed with anger as he started to pack his things. His intentions were clear now. He didn't feel like staying in the hostel. This place, the whole campus had no value for him anymore. He hated to be around the places in the campus where Kavya and he had spent time together. The canteen, park, roads, shops, fountain, stairs…he just wanted to go away from all these and never come back.

He decided to ditch the Goa trip with his friends and go home.

Later in the evening, when everyone was asleep, he sneaked out. He didn't even bother to bid his roommates adieu; he knew that, if they saw him, they would try to talk him out of it. It was the last thing he wanted.

A part of him knew for sure that he would not come back for his last semester. This made his heart even colder. The farther he walked, the harder the steps became. Yet, he dragged his luggage and kept walking until he reached the exit gate.

When he approached the exit gate, he remembered the first time he had entered the campus. He had been a teenager, eager and ambitious to start a new journey—one that he had never imagined would end like this.

The taxi was waiting at the gate. He walked straight to it and didn't look back.

There was a strange silence inside him. For a moment, he went blank. He was unable to believe that he was actually doing this. He wished it were a dream but it wasn't.

The driver started the car and the jolt woke Rehan up from his numbness.

"Where to?" the cab driver asked him.

Rehan kept quiet for a second. Then, "Railway station," he said.

~Bhubaneswar

After a thirty-six-hour-long journey, Rehan reached his hometown.

As he climbed down from the train, he heard people chattering in Odia, his native language. He felt at home. When he stepped out of the railway station, the familiar sight of his hometown, smells and chaos took him back to his past. As a teen, he used to roam these streets. He felt a little relieved to be back home. For a moment, he forgot about his pain. Walking among his own people brought a smile to his face. He felt refreshed.

It was nine in the morning. He took a cab to his home.

While he was in the cab, he switched on his phone. There were thirteen missed calls and a bunch of messages. He hoped to see Kavya's name in the notifications but it was just his friends. They were concerned about him. He ignored the messages and looked out of the window. The fresh wintry air blew over his face, making him realize just how much he had missed the city.

The cab took him through various back roads and alleys. He reached home in half an hour. As soon as he rang the bell, his mom answered the door. She was wearing a sari and her hands were wet. Rehan could smell the curry she was cooking. It smelled good.

"Rehan!" she smiled as she gave him a tight hug. "I thought you were going to Goa," she said, a perplexed look on her face.

"No. I cancelled," Rehan said, avoiding eye contact.

"Why *bacha*? You sounded so excited on the phone when you told us about your Goa trip. What happened?" She sounded a bit worried.

"I had to complete a project. So, I cancelled." He put an arm around her and went inside. "I'm starving, mom." He tried to take her mind off the Goa topic. He was also really hungry, and the smell of curry was making his stomach rumble.

"You go freshen up first. I'll get something for you," her mom said.

She didn't buy Rehan's excuse but she let it go for now. He was never much into studies, and ditching fun for studies didn't sound like something he would do. She decided to wait till he felt comfortable enough to tell her.

Rehan's dad was at the dining table, having breakfast along with his younger brother. Rehan went up to hug him. His dad got up from the chair and hugged him back. He also asked him about the Goa trip and was given the same excuse.

"So, how did your exams go?" his dad asked.

Rehan knew he didn't do well in the exams but he couldn't say that to his dad's face. So, he lied: "Exams went well."

He sat down with his dad and brother to have breakfast.

Later that day, when Rehan was in his room alone, his mom walked in. He was sitting on the bed silently, looking out of the window. She sensed that something was wrong with her son. She sat beside him and asked him about it. "What happened, Rehan? Are you worried about something?"

Rehan wasn't expecting this. He was a bit surprised. He couldn't think of any good responses at the moment. So, he made something up about the exams. He said he didn't do well in the exams so he was upset about that. Luckily, that was a good enough lie for his mom to believe. She brushed his hair as she tried to console him.

"Everything is going to be alright, *beta*."

"Hmm." Rehan nodded. Deep down, he knew everything was messed up. It was not going to be alright any time soon.

Days passed. Rehan stayed mostly at home. Usually, when he used to come home during vacations, he would go out and meet his friends three or four times a week. This time, he barely walked out of his room. This seemed a little odd to her mother but she thought Rehan was still upset about his studies, so she didn't interfere.

Rehan sat in his room all day, and came out only to eat. He would sit in his bed the whole time and look at the pictures on his laptop. They were all of Kavya. He read all their chats on the phone. It was getting worse day by day. He was not getting over her at all. Instead, he was drowning in her memory. The loneliness was killing him.

A few days later, the results were out. His friends from college were talking about it on the WhatsApp group. When Rehan woke up, he saw their messages. A chill ran down his spine. The days were already bad; now, with the results coming out, they would be much worse.

He was afraid to check his results. Still, he opened the website and logged in. He had failed in five out of six subjects. This was the first time in his life that he had failed so miserably at something. He felt extremely bad about himself. Later, a lot of his friends messaged him, asking about his results—which made it even worse.

He still wasn't over Kavya; the results made him feel even more depressed. With everything that was going on around him lately, he considered himself a loser. That's what he thought he was. He lost at love. He lost at college. Now, if his parents saw the results, he would lose in front of them as well. He felt that all doors were closing behind him and he couldn't see a way out. He had no motivation left.

He stayed in bed until his dad came and told him to wake up and join him for breakfast.

While eating, all he was thinking about was his next step. He now had a total of six failed subjects, including this semester's five. This meant spending an extra year in college. The thought of one more year at college, with Kavya studying there as well, was going to be torture for him.

After breakfast, he went back to his room and thought about the possibilities of going back to college. There were none, because he had absolutely no interest in going back there. Secondly, he didn't want to waste his dad's money anymore. Thirdly, he didn't have the courage to tell his dad about his failure. He sat on his bed, holding his head in his hands.

"What will I do now? Where will I go if I don't go back to college?" he asked himself.

He was terrified. He felt like he didn't have a pinch of self-confidence left in him. He weighed his options to get out of this situation.

"You can always look for a job." The answer came from within.

"But I'm not even a graduate yet."

"So what? You don't have to be a graduate to be something."

"What do you mean?"

"Do what you do best."

"That's it?"

"Yes. Ask yourself, what is it that you are good at?"

"I don't know. Photography, maybe."

"Thought so!"

As soon as his inner self replied, he looked at his camera, untouched since the day he had returned home. In the ocean of disappointment and negativity he was drowning in, he saw a drop of hope.

That day, Rehan decided to go out and meet some of his school friends.

When we are pushed to the limit, we don't care about the outcome—we just follow our instincts. Don't we?

That's what Rehan did. He called and set up a meeting with his photographer friends in town. There were only two of them: Dhruv and Shrey.

The three of them went back a long way. They had been very good friends in school. After school, Rehan went for IIT coaching while Dhruv and Shrey stayed on in the town. They kept in touch on social media but their paths eventually diverged. Since school days, the three of them had loved photography. Back then, only Shrey had had a camera. Now, both Shrey and Dhruv had dropped out of college and running their own studio business. Rehan hoped they might help him get a gig that could help him kick-start a new life.

Rehan planned to meet them at the coffee shop in the mall. He reached half an hour earlier.

Dhruv arrived there first, followed by Shrey after fifteen minutes. They talked about their lives and the good old memories for a bit. Rehan was looking for a moment to put in his point about a job. They talked and laughed, with pauses in between. During one such pause, Rehan said, "Guys, I need your help."

"Sure..." Shrey said. "Yeah, tell us." Dhruv also joined in. They sat up straight as they became serious.

"It might sound a little weird but I'm really serious about it. Lately, I've been thinking of dropping out of college but I don't have any lead to my future yet. I don't need this coding shit in my life...so I thought...maybe I could do photography just like you guys, and be a professional. I had good experience in it. I need a gig urgently. Will you guys help me get one?" Rehan said.

"You are dropping out?" Dhruv was surprised.

"Why?" Shrey asked.

"It's a long story guys. I will tell you about it later. For now please help me find a gig. It's urgent," Rehan said.

"Okay. We will." They nodded.

For the next three days, Rehan waited for them to call him but they didn't. He was getting desperate so he called Dhruv.

"Hey," Rehan said.

"Hi Rehan," Dhruv replied.

"Where are you, man?"

"I'm at a shoot location."

"Sorry to interrupt you, man, I just called to know whether you found anything or not."

"No dude. Nothing yet. But I will call you once I get something."

He called Shrey but got the same response. However, Shrey did give him a lead for the interim period.

"Hey, listen. Why don't you put together a portfolio in the meantime?" Shrey suggested. "I'm sure you have some amazing clicks."

Rehan thought that was a good idea. He thanked him and put the phone down.

After dinner, Rehan went into his room, opened his laptop and started picking out his best works. He went through all the pictures he had clicked in the last two years—including all the events, festivals, hostel life, nature and candid. He went through at least a couple of thousands of pictures, and it took him a few hours to sort them out.

At around three in the morning, he finished looking through all the pictures on his laptop. He got up, walked to the table and picked up the camera. He had to go through the SD card for the rest of the pictures. They were mainly of Kavya's sister's wedding. He didn't want to see them again but he remembered that he had clicked some beautiful pictures that day. So, he inserted the SD card into the laptop and opened the pictures. It started with a smiling picture of Kavya. He looked at it for a moment. Before he drowned in the memories again, he swiped and moved on to the rest. He copied the ones he liked. Suddenly, he saw a picture that reminded him of something. It was the picture of a girl in a long white *kurta*; she had a camera in her hand and a tattoo on her neck. This rang a bell—he remembered that she was the photographer who had covered Riya's wedding. He recalled that they had had a little chat. She had also given him her card, in case he wanted to join her team. A wave of energy ran through him. He got up and searched for her visiting card in his bag. He found it in the first pocket.

'Tulika Mahajan' was the name. There was her number and email id. Mailing her and waiting for response would have taken a lot of time and he was not in a position to waste any. So he texted her on WhatsApp. He wrote: *Hey. Remember me? Rehan, the guy from IIT, we met in West Bengal two months back, in a wedding. You gave me your card. I need your help.*

He sent it. Then, he continued working on his portfolio. He uploaded all the pictures. There were hundreds of them. It was taking time, so he decided to play around with his phone. As soon as he picked up the phone, it beeped. A new message had arrived.

Tulika had replied: *Hey dude. Of course I remember. Tell me, how can I help?*

It was three-thirty in the morning. Rehan was surprised.

I wasn't expecting a reply so soon though. You've not slept yet? He wrote back.

At a party.

Oh! Okay. Enjoy. I will ping you later.

You can call me later in the afternoon.

Okay. Sure.

The next afternoon, Rehan called her. She picked up his call right away. For the first few seconds, Rehan couldn't think of anything to say to her.

Then, he said, "Hi."

"Hello?" Tulika replied. "Who's this?"

"Rehan! I texted you in the morning, at four... you were at a party."

"Oh yeah! Hi Rehan. What's up?"

"How was the party last night?"

"It was good."

"Nice."

"So tell me…"

"I saw all your clicks on Facebook. They are beautiful. You are really talented."

"Thanks."

"I loved the rain pictures. Specially the one you had taken at that wedding—of me and my friend."

"Oh yeah. That one. I also love that picture. It reminds me of how I used to get drenched in the rain," she said. She paused and then continued, "Anyway, you didn't tell me what help you wanted."

"So I…uh…know this is kind of awkward but I needed a gig and I remembered that we had talked about it that day. So, as I was reaching out to people for help, I thought, why not call someone I know?"

"A gig? What happened to your studies?"

"Urm…I dropped out."

"Really?"

"Yeah."

"That's cool."

Rehan was surprised by her reaction. Unlike Dhruv and Shrey, she took it unexpectedly well.

"So, would you be able to get me one?" he asked.

"Well…I might have something but let me check with my team first. I'll get back to you. Okay?"

"Yeah. Sure."

This gave Rehan some hope. He wondered if Tulika would be able to help him. He waited for her to call back.

Half an hour later, she called back.

"Congratulations! I got you a job," she said.

"Really? Thank you so much, Tulika!" Rehan was very excited. The tiny ray of hope shone over the darkness.

"Don't thank me yet. You will have to come to Mumbai first. My team wants to meet you before they hand over the assignment."

"Okay, no problem. I'll be there."

"You have to be here by this weekend. Can you make it?"

The weekend was just three days away. It was sooner than he had expected. But he wasn't going to lose this opportunity.

"Yeah, I will be there."

"Perfect."

So, everything was set. He finally got the opportunity he wanted. Now, he didn't have to go back to college. Things were eventually looking up for Rehan. He took a deep breath and looked out of the window. The sky seemed bluer than on a normal afternoon. He heard the melodious chirping of the birds. He smiled.

Everything was fine, except for one thing. He didn't know how to tell his parents about it. He wasn't sure whether his father would let him drop out of college just like that. He knew they wouldn't take it well. So, he lied to them that he was going to Mumbai to attend his friend's sister's marriage. He also said that he would be leaving for college from Mumbai itself, as there were only a few days left from the holidays. His parents believed him. They also wanted him to go out and enjoy, as he had been so reserved for the last few days.

Finally, the day arrived.

Rehan was at the railway station with his parents and younger brother. They had come to see him off for his last semester at college. Rehan kept his luggage inside the train, and stood on the platform with his dad. Suddenly, his dad put his hand on Rehan's shoulder and said with a smile, "The next time when we will meet on this platform you will be a graduate."

Rehan's heart sank. He looked into his dad's eyes—he saw trust and belief, which he was going to break. It wasn't easy for him to lie to his parents, but going back to college wasn't an option anymore. He just nodded silently.

The train blew its horn. Rehan climbed up the stairs and stood at the door. He waved to his family as the train slowly moved out of the platform. He stood there, gazing at the crowd. As the wheels moved faster, people started to fade away from sight. Finally, he turned around and went to his seat. He knew that his father would find out the truth one day. For now, a new life awaited him.

~Mumbai

The next morning, Rehan reached Mumbai. He had never been to that city before, although he had heard a lot about it from his 'Mumbaikar' friend, Srikaanth. As soon as he stepped off the train, the first thing that hit him was the chaos. Everyone was rushing. Life appeared to be faster than usual. The weather was moderate but a bit humid. He walked out with his bags and saw a giant line of cabs outside the station. He took one of them and followed the address that Tulika had given him. It was in Andheri East.

The traffic was moving slowly, so he decided to call Tulika.

"Hey! Good morning," Rehan greeted her.

"Hi. Morning. Did you reach?" she asked.

"Yeah. In a cab. Heading to the address you had sent me."

"Oh cool. I'll be there in half an hour. Let me know if you reach there before me. I'll make the arrangements for you."

"Yeah. Sure."

"And listen don't pay the taxi driver more than two hundred. Those bloody idiots tend to rob newcomers," she said.

Rehan had put the phone on speaker as he wasn't able to hear properly in the traffic. Apparently, Tulika's voice did reach the driver's ears.

"Okay," he replied awkwardly, looking at the driver.

Deep down, he smiled, as Tulika's caring nature touched his heart.

Coming to Mumbai was a dream come true for Rehan. For a moment, he couldn't believe all this was happening for real—he was grateful to Tulika for helping him out. *How many strangers do you know, who would do such things? Maybe it was the artists' bond that spoke for them. As far as I've known in my life, until now, artists always support each other.*

Rehan reached the place. It was a thirteen-storied building and the office was on the fifth floor. He jumped into the elevator.

He reached the office. The board outside read 'Camgicians'; it was written in fine cursive font. It was a combination of the words 'camera' and 'magicians,' as he interpreted it. He liked the place. Just as he was about to enter the office, he got a call from Tulika.

"Hey. Where are you?" she asked.

"I'm just outside the office."

"Okay. Wait a second. I am coming. I'm in the lift."

"Okay."

When the lift's doors opened, Tulika stepped out. She didn't look anything like he remembered her. At the wedding, she had worn a traditional white dress. Here she was, rocking a crop top and distressed jeans. She looked much sexier than she had at the wedding.

Rehan smiled.

"Rehan?" she said.

"Yes."

"Hi." She shook his hand.

"Hi"

"So, how was the journey?"

"Good."

"Come on. Let's go inside," she said as she led the way into the office.

"Sure." Rehan followed her.

They walked into the office. *If you could call it an office.* The walls were painted in pastel colors, and beautiful photographs were hung from them. There were cushions everywhere and people were working in groups, either sitting on the floor or on beanbags. A couple of people were playing table tennis in one corner. Another corner had a drum set and a guitar. It looked more like a place to hang out than an office.

Rehan followed Tulika to a bigger, closed room that was called the 'prism.' A few people who were inside greeted Rehan.

Tulika introduced him to the team members and founder of the group. He talked to them and told them about his photography experiences. All of them were a bit shocked on hearing about his IIT background. People don't expect IITians to drop out and pick up random gigs. Maybe that's why he became so popular among the team members right away.

His first assignment was in Mumbai itself—he had to cover a wedding. Tulika took on the responsibility of polishing up his skills before he took it on. Rehan was happy to hear that. Everyone was very welcoming.

Rehan stayed there for the whole day. He had called his friend, Srikaanth, at some point, and requested that he stay with him for a few days. Without any hesitation, Srikaanth welcomed Rehan to his home.

Before leaving, Rehan went to Tulika and thanked her for everything. She smiled and patted his shoulder. She had a strange confidence within her. She seemed bold and independent. Rehan admired her even more.

While he was leaving, Tulika reminded him to come to the studio at ten the next morning. They would have a session to work on his skills, and then a polishing session. She also asked if he had any place to stay, to which Rehan said he did.

"If you run into any problem, call me. You are welcome to stay at my place," Tulika said as she waved goodbye.

Rehan took a taxi to Srikaanth's place.

After dinner, Srikaanth and Rehan went inside his room to chat. The door was partially open.

"So, you're in Mumbai all of a sudden. What's up with you, man?" Srikaanth asked.

"Yeah. I don't think you are gonna like it." Rehan made a sour face.

"What?"

"Well, I'm not going back to college."

"What? Then where are you going?"

"Nowhere. I'm staying here in Mumbai itself."

"Are you dropping out of college?"

"Yes."

"I can't believe it. Are you serious?"

"Yes. One hundred percent."

"But what are you gonna do here? How are you gonna survive? This isn't Indore or Bhubaneswar. It's Mumbai man. Most people spend half of their salaries in paying rents and bills."

"Well, I got a job."

"What? Where?"

"I joined a photography group. They are gonna send me for assignments. My first one is on the twenty-seventh of this month."

"Photography? How much are they going to pay you?"

"I don't know. Haven't thought of it. But it's better than going to college and spend one more year there for nothing."

"I thought it was your last year?"

"I failed in five subjects this semester."

"Five? What happened man? You were so steady with your grades each year. How did you slip this time?"

"I don't know, and I don't want to discuss about it either. It's in the past and I would like to keep it that way. I have already chosen my life now."

"Wow. Good for you, Rehan. You really have the guts to drop out. I just read about them in novels and seen them in movies."

"You know what? You should also drop out and join a band. You'll become a rock star—I'm telling you."

"Are you mad? I can't do that. Even if I want to, my mom and dad won't let me do this. They have already planned for my MS."

"Dude, ask yourself. What do you really want to be?"

Srikaanth was thinking about that when his mom called him. Her voice seemed to come from close by. It seemed she was standing right outside the room. Rehan was afraid that she might have heard his dropping-out and failing-in-five-subjects comments. Which actually turned out to be true. Srikaanth's mom was not a smooth talker. She told her son loud and clear that Rehan should be gone from their house the next day.

Well, he couldn't blame her. She was right in a way. Who would want their kids to be friends with an academic failure? No one in India, at least. Still, he felt bad. Srikaanth argued with his mom but she shut him up. Moms do it just like that, with the snap of a finger.

Srikaanth went back into the room with a dejected face. Rehan comforted him up and told him it was good for both of them.

Before they went to sleep Srikaanth mentioned Kavya's name and asked how it was going between them. Rehan heard him but pretended to have fallen asleep. From the moment Rehan had landed in Mumbai, he had tried to not think about Kavya, and it was going pretty well. Now that Srikaanth had mentioned her name, all he could think about was her.

The next day, Rehan left early in the morning with his baggage. He reached the studio before ten. He had never been in a professional studio before. The one he was standing in was a huge room with all kinds of lighting equipment, backdrops and cameras. He was fascinated. Tulika came in a bit late, at around 10.30.

"Sorry. You know how Mumbai's traffic is," she said. Then, she glanced at the bags by his side and asked about them. He told her about what had happened the previous night at his friend's house.

"It's alright. Don't worry. You can stay with me until you get your own place," she consoled him. Rehan wanted to live alone for a while, so he respectfully declined and said that he would find a place for himself.

Later, they did a little session on camera and lighting. Tulika taught him a few basic things, which Rehan later used in his first assignment. His innovative ideas of framing, lighting experiments, surreal manipulations and concepts of pictures were really good. This gave him a good name in the team. He soon received more and more projects. He became so busy in life that, in the blink of an eye, a year passed by.

One day, his dad called him to ask about the convocation ceremony. Rehan had been hiding the truth from him over the last year but he finally decided to tell him the truth. Eventually, he would find out, so there was no point in hiding it anymore.

His dad shouted at him angrily and cut the phone call. He stopped talking to him. Rehan understood. He knew this had to happen someday. He began to send all his work to his mom, who showed them to his dad.

Given his creative ideas and concepts, Rehan got offers for fashion shoots as well. Slowly, he climbed the steps and started shooting for bigger brands. It took time but the outcome was worth it. He became popular among the fashion circle and started covering high-profile weddings and photo-shoots. It took him five years but he made it to the top. He could no longer see the Rehan who had failed at life.

His dad ignored him at first but, eventually, when Rehan settled down, bought his own car and got his name featured in magazines, his anger melted away. Success was all he had wanted for his boy and Rehan had achieved it. His dad felt proud of him.

Now, Rehan was a well-known Bollywood photographer. Fame had helped him come out of his misery but he wasn't fully healed yet.

On that day, his soul had been shattered; he was never able to glue the pieces back again.

Through the five years of his journey, he felt the pain every single day but channeled it into hard work.

Chapter 7
The Confession

19 January 2016

Rehan was lying on the bed, staring at the ceiling. It was nine in the morning. The sun had come up. The curtains blocked the light from falling directly on his face. He turned to his right and opened his eyes. The bottle of whisky and half-filled glass were the first things that he saw. The room was brightly lit by the morning light but his eyes hadn't adjusted yet. He blinked a few times; his eyes were red and watery. He looked pretty sick. His head was throbbing with pain. He massaged his head with his fingers, pulled himself up and sat on the edge of the bed. He looked at the glass again. The whisky inside it seemed to have settled; the brown surface was calm, just like the room. He grabbed the phone lying by his side. There were nine missed calls. Seven of them were from Tulika and two from an unknown number. Rehan took the phone, got up and stumbled towards the kitchen, where he drank a glass of water to cure some of his hangover.

On the way to the kitchen, he called Tulika.

"Good morning," he greeted her.

"Morning," Tulika replied. "Where were you last night? You didn't pick up my calls?"

"I had slept off early because of a headache." Rehan didn't tell her about the alcohol. He didn't want her to know about what had happened the previous night.

"How is it now?" She seemed concerned.

"Feeling better. When's your flight?"

"Boarding now. In the queue."

"Did you get any sleep?"

"Not really. I'll take a nap in the flight. Luckily, they've booked me in business class."

"Okay. That sounds good."

"Yeah. Okay, I gotto go. You take care."

"You too."

"I'll call you when I land."

Rehan came back to his room with a glass of water. He took out a strip of Disprin tablets from his drawer and tossed one into the glass. His head was pounding, as if somebody was playing drums inside it. He drank the water and fell on the bed again.

A few minutes later, he took his phone and checked the messages on WhatsApp. There were a few group messages—some friends from work had pinged him. There was also a message from an unknown number. It was a girl—Rehan could tell that much from the display picture. And a beautiful one at that. He was curious. He opened the picture. It was Kavya. He was a bit surprised. The number on WhatsApp looked familiar to him. He checked his call log and realized it was the same number he had gotten two missed calls from earlier. He checked her messages. It read: *Hey. Kavya here. Tried calling you twice in the evening, you were busy I guess. Let's meet at Harry's bar at 8 tonight. The place is in Hiranandani, I'll send you the location. Let me know if you can come.*

Rehan read it, he looked up and stared at the whisky bottle. "Not again! No!" said his mind.

He was in a dilemma. He couldn't decide if he should go or not. His finger hovered over the keypad as he decided what to write. He looked around the room while trying to compose a reply.

Why did she want to meet him now? Was there any part of him left unbroken? Did she want to rip out his heart and tear it apart—again? Or did she want something else?

All these years, he had tried to suppress those memories, keep them at the back of his mind and not let them affect his life. With Kavya coming back, those memories resurfaced. The wound that he had kept hidden all these years was exposed; the dark feelings came rushing back. After all that had happened, he couldn't just go and meet her like that. No—he owed himself that much self-respect.

He decided not to go.

He quickly wrote: *No. I can't come.* Before he sent it, he waited. He closed his eyes. All his instincts were telling him to press the 'send' button but he couldn't. He erased the message. He wasn't sure of what he was typing. A part of him knew that he wanted to meet Kavya again, and it didn't let him say 'no.' It was like choosing between two doors—one with a tiger and another with a ghost inside.

He remembered that he had stood in front of these doors before. That time, when he had made up his mind to move to Mumbai, he was worried about what his dad would say. He had had only two choices then—listen to his mind and stay with family, or follow his heart and go to Mumbai.

Most people fail to listen to their heart and remain stuck in their lives, forever repenting their choice. It is not always easy to follow your heart. You have to have the strength to do so, and the willingness to pull it off. It is not something everybody can do.

Rehan had listened to his heart. He had chosen the ghost.

The heart always knows what you want, even when you don't know it.

If he hadn't come to Mumbai that day, worrying about the odds, he wouldn't have succeeded at all.

He realized that he was afraid of his past with Kavya, and of getting hurt again. However, there could be another side to the story—things were not black-and-white as he thought them to be.

He decided to see her.

Sure. I'll be there, he wrote back as he chose the ghost again.

~Evening

When Rehan reached Harry's bar, it was very crowded. Every table was full. People were drinking, laughing and shouting. Rehan felt that he didn't belong there. He had been to only one or two bars in the last two years. So, it was a little awkward for him to walk in amid all those strangers.

He dodged a few girls who were carrying giant pitchers, and a group of people who were dancing like monkeys by the side of their table. "What kind of crazy animals are these people?" he thought to himself.

He looked around for Kavya. His white shirt reflected the neon light coming from the dance floor. The music was too loud to make a call, so he just kept searching for her.

Suddenly, he heard someone shouting out his name from a corner of the bar. He turned around. There she was. She looked beautiful in black jeans and a black top. He waved back, and walked over to her.

"Hi," he said as he reached the bar counter.

"Hey," she smiled.

Rehan smiled, too, but it was just a reflex. "So... what's up?"

"Just came from work," Kavya said.

Rehan nodded. "Oh, where do you work?" he asked.

"At Kailash Business Park in Vikhroli. It's nearby."

"Okay. Nice."

Meanwhile, the bartender asked Rehan for his order. He ordered a mocktail for himself.

"So, software and all huh?" he asked Kavya.

"Yeah. Product manager at an e-commerce company."

"Wow."

"No. Nothing's wow. Life is so fucked up with the job. No time for family or for myself. Every weekend, I find myself coming here to enjoy with some of my friends. I am trying not to lose my sanity."

"Really?" Rehan was slowly getting comfortable; he didn't feel awkward anymore.

Have you experienced this? When someone opens up about their life and puts forward their problems, the conversation is no longer awkward.

"Where are your friends?" Rehan asked.

"Urm…it's just me today." She quickly downed a shot of vodka. "So, how's your life going?"

"It's good…I live nearby…work's good…. I keep roaming all over the world for shoots. In fact, I'm flying to Paris next week for a fashion shoot…. So, yeah…everything is good." Rehan paused after every line. Though he wasn't awkward anymore, he still wasn't ready to open up in front of her. It was Kavya he was talking to—the girl who had broken his heart.

"So, you live with friends or alone?" Kavya asked.

"Urm…alone. I live alone," Rehan replied.

He didn't know why he lied. He lived with Tulika. What was going on in his mind?

Kavya nodded as she took another vodka shot.

"Rehan, I wanted to tell you something." She looked into his eyes for a moment and then looked away. She asked the bartender to line up more shots.

"How many of those have you taken till now?" Rehan asked.

"Only four." She held up four fingers.

"When did you start drinking?" As per his knowledge, she never ever drank while they were together back in college.

"Long back. In college."

"Oh!"

The word 'college' made Rehan sit up straight. It brought back bittersweet memories. Yet, he recovered and kept the conversation going.

"You were saying something…" he prompted.

"Yeah…yeah," she stammered while she took another shot.

"You are drooling already. You shouldn't take any more of those. If you want, we can go out somewhere. We'll sit and talk," Rehan suggested.

"No. I like the music and the vibe here."

"Are you sure?"

"Yes"

"Okay."

Kavya seemed nervous. Well, whatever it was, she couldn't talk about it. Maybe that's why she was drinking so much—to get some liquid courage. Her eyes darted here and there, and she gave a few awkward smiles.

Rehan had already sensed that she was not comfortable. She looked very tense and her body language told the rest.

Suddenly, she looked right into his eyes—those dark grey eyes she had missed all these years. Her lips started to quiver when she prepared to speak—just then, Rehan's phone started to ring. It was right there, on the table. Rehan turned to look at the phone; it caught Kavya's attention as well. Her lips glued shut as she paused. He took the phone and got off the chair.

"I'll be right back.... And don't take any more of those shots."

Kavya nodded.

Rehan went outside; it was Tulika on the phone.

"Hey, how was the day?" Rehan asked.

"Hi, it was good. Went to the shoot location today. Met up with some new people in the field. Had chicken in my favorite restaurant. It was really an awesome day."

"That's good. Seems like you've had a pretty fun day."

"Yeah. It was fun. By the way, are you out?"

She might have heard the noise. The street around Harry's bar was a busy one. Cars, bikes and people were coming and going.

"Yeah. Came to meet an old friend from college."

"Okay then, you have fun. I gotto go to bed. I'm really tired and I have to wake up really early tomorrow…shoot is in the morning."

"Sure. Goodnight, and take care."

"You too."

Rehan walked back into the bar. The music was louder and everyone was dancing beside their tables. Rehan reached the bar counter. He saw Kavya had already gulped down five more shots. She was so drunk that she couldn't stop giggling.

Rehan told the bartender to remove the glasses and not bring any more drinks.

"Are you alright?" he asked her.

"Yeah. I'm fine."

"You don't look fine."

"Don't worry. I'm fine."

As she climbed down from her seat, she stumbled. She was about to lose her balance when Rehan grabbed her.

She mumbled, "I'm fine. I'm fine."

"I think we should go," Rehan said, and sat her down on the sofa nearby. He went to the bar to pay the bill.

While the bartender swiped his card, he looked at Kavya. She was still jabbering away.

Rehan helped her out of the bar. Kavya couldn't even walk straight. Rehan had to put her arms around his shoulder and drag her to the parking lot.

When they reached the parking lot, Rehan called her name twice but she didn't listen. He gently patted her cheek a couple of times but she didn't respond.

He walked her to his car and sat her down on the back seat. He took her phone out of her pocket. He thought he could find some contact and call them but her phone was locked. Rehan didn't know the password, so he tried waking her up again. She lay flat on the back seat and did not respond. Rehan tried calling Anjali but she didn't pick up. He felt it wasn't nice to call her again at such a late hour. So, he put away his phone.

He walked back and forth beside the car. He was thinking about where to drop her. He didn't know her address. He had no girlfriends in town, and neither of their families lived nearby.

Finally, he made a decision. He got into the car. He had no choice but to take her to his flat.

He drove slowly so that she wouldn't slide down from the seat. He kept looking back frequently to make sure she was okay. Also, he was scared of the police.

Since it was a weekend night, the police checked closely for drink-and-drive cases. Rehan was worried that, if they saw Kavya lying down in the back seat like that, they might get the wrong idea—and he could get into a lot of trouble. So, he drove carefully, checking every signal he came across. It took him forty-five minutes to get to his place, which was barely fifteen minutes away.

They reached his apartment. Rehan parked his car and carried Kavya to the lift. After they entered the flat, Rehan picked her up and walked towards Tulika's room—when something hit him. Earlier, he had told her that he lived alone. It wouldn't take her long to find out that it was a girl's room. So, he turned around and walked into his room.

He laid her down on his bed. She was still blacked out. Rehan sat on the sofa and looked at her. She was breathing peacefully. He stretched himself out on the sofa.

Sometime around midnight, Rehan heard Kavya mumbling something. He woke up and went near her. She was talking in her sleep. Rehan gently caressed her forehead and whispered in her ear to go back to sleep. As he tucked her hair around her ear, he heard her say his name.

"Rehan. Is that you?" she asked, eyes closed.

"Yes."

She grasped his hand and pulled it towards her chest. She held it tightly and kissed it. Rehan didn't know what was happening. He sat there beside her, clueless.

She kissed his hand again as she turned towards her left, where Rehan was sitting. She started speaking.

"Rehan, I want to tell you something. Before I start, I request you not to judge me. I've kept it in my heart since the last five years and I can't keep it in anymore now." She paused and continued, "Remember Riya's wedding? The day when we were together for the last time? Later that day, I overheard Riya talking to dad. Dad was screaming at her—he had cut her off from our family and declared her dead for him, because she was marrying a guy from another caste. She was crying. I felt so bad for her. That was the moment when I made the biggest mistake of my life. Riya was marrying someone who was not of her caste but I was in love with someone who was from a different religion altogether. I freaked out. I cried all night thinking about losing you and losing my family. I didn't know what to do but I had to make a decision. I chose my family. I couldn't lose my mom and dad. I was scared. So, I distanced myself and lied to you about not loving you. I accepted the fact that destiny was hard on me. I thought I did the right thing but I didn't know that destiny would come back and bite me even harder." She sobbed.

"Later that year, dad lost almost everything in business and went into depression. He had a heart attack and needed surgery. All our relatives, everybody backed out. No one was ready to help us either mentally or financially. I told Riya about it. Aditya and she came to Chandigarh right away. Aditya had many contacts. He made arrangements for the best doctors in the country and took care of the surgery. They were at the hospital the whole time. When dad woke up, he realized his mistake and apologized to them. He not only accepted Aditya but stood up to everyone in our family who were against Riya's marriage. He even became open to love marriages. That heart attack changed dad. He became a whole new person.

"That was the worst day for me. I was glad that dad had changed but I cursed myself for losing you. I wanted to call you. One day, I gathered all my courage and called you, but your number was switched off. I tried many times after that but it was switched off every time. Then, I realized you might have changed your number. I tried to find you on social media but you were not active anywhere. Then, two years later, I saw your picture with some film stars on Facebook. I read about you on Google and I learned that you had become a celebrity photographer.

"I was glad that you had achieved your dream. I used to read each and every article about you in the newspapers. I understood that you were happy in your life so I tried to move on. But I couldn't, Rehan. I couldn't get over you. Every time I went out with somebody, the inner me would poke me about how much wrong I did to you. That feeling killed me each and every day. I promised myself that I would not think about you anymore. Then, we met in the café the other day and I couldn't stop myself from falling for you all over again.

"I had lied to you about not loving you. The truth is that I have always loved you, since the first day we met, since the first time you touched me in the cab, since the first time we kissed. I have never stopped loving you Rehan. I hate myself for losing you to fear. I curse myself every day. I don't know about how you feel about me now. You might have found someone in your life. It's okay if you are over me but at least forgive me so that I can live my life without any guilt. I'm sorry Rehan…I'm really sorry. I'm sorry. I'm sorr…" She drifted off again.

Rehan was surprised by everything she had just said. It was quite a shock for him. He had been wrong—she loved him. The anger and frustration deep inside his heart melted away in seconds. His view towards Kavya changed. He was mature now, so he understood her circumstances, the pain and heartbreak she must have gone through. He found his emotions again, locked away somewhere in a corner of his heart. The long lost love was sparked again. A strange smile blossomed on his face. He looked at Kavya; she was sleeping by his side, holding his hands close to her chest. He didn't want to pull his hand away, so he just sat there for a while. He was lost in his own world. Every word rang in his ears. He gently stroked her hair, covered her with a blanket. That night, he dreamt about a new future—a beautiful one, with Kavya.

There is a thin line between love and hate. In this case, it was Kavya's confession. Later, when Kavya fell asleep Rehan slowly pulled his hand away. He kissed her on her forehead and moved to the couch. He had a smile on his face when he slept.

The next morning, Kavya woke up early. She had a mild headache when she woke up. The first thing she saw was Rehan sleeping on the couch. She didn't quite understand. Where was she? Why were they in the same room?

She tried to recall what had happened last night but all she could remember was that Rehan had gone out to take a call. She didn't remember anything that had happened after that.

She looked around. It was a nice room but it didn't seem familiar to her. She got up from the bed and went to the table. She saw some pictures, a camera, a laptop and few books.

There was a picture of Rehan on the mantle. "So it's his room," she thought to herself. She pulled the curtains apart and looked through the window. The sun had come up; it was a beautiful view. She turned around and looked at Rehan. He was sleeping like a baby.

She searched for her bag. It was on the chair. She pulled out her journal from her bag and wrote down about being in Rehan's room.

She was writing when she heard the phone ring. She looked on the bed. It was Rehan's phone, kept next to the pillow. The caller id read 'Tulika.' She wondered who it was.

"Might be some friend or colleague," she thought. She put her journal back in her bag and jumped onto the bed.

The phone beeped again—a text message. The message showed up on the screen: *Good news. I had the trip cut short. Will be reaching there before noon. I missed you. Hope my room is untouched.*

Kavya didn't understand. Though she suspected something about the 'I missed you' part, it was still unclear.

She quickly got up and walked out. She saw another room just beside Rehan's. She opened the door and walked in. It seemed like a girl's room. She opened the wardrobe and saw a bunch of ladies garments hanging inside. She stood there for a while and recalled that Rehan had told her that he lived alone. *Why did he lie to her?*

She went back to Rehan's room. Something was going on in her mind—whatever it was, it wasn't good. She thought Rehan might have moved on, and felt awkward about telling that to her. She stayed quiet and calm though she felt angry and sad. She was sitting on the bed, lost in her thoughts, when Rehan woke up.

"Hey…" he said, stretching his arms. His voice dripped with love.

"Hi…" Kavya replied in a subdued tone.

"When did you wake up?"

"Just a moment ago."

Rehan got up and went over to her.

"Did you sleep well?" he asked, looking into her eyes. This seemed a bit strange to Kavya. She didn't get it. Why was Rehan being so sweet all of a sudden?

"Hmmm."

"Tea or coffee?" Rehan asked.

"Coffee."

"Okay." Rehan gave her a wide smile and walked to the kitchen.

He thought about the things Kavya had said last night. He giggled while making coffee. He had never felt this light-hearted before.

Rehan came back with two cups of coffee, and sat down beside her. They both took a sip.

"So, this is your place?" Kavya asked while she looked around the room and took another sip of the coffee.

"Yeah. You were blackout drunk yesterday. Your phone was locked so I couldn't contact any of your friends. Anjali didn't pick up the phone. So my last option was to bring you here. So I did. Hope you don't mind."

"No. It's okay. Thanks." She took another sip of the coffee. "So you live alone, huh?"

Rehan kept quiet for a moment. Then he said, "Yeah." Before Kavya could say anything Rehan spoke up: "Listen Kavya, the day we broke up, I was totally heartbroken and I never wished to see your face again. But deep down, a part of me always loved you. There wasn't a day when I didn't remember you. But the way you walked away made me grow mad at you. But that was only my part of the story. You never even told me yours until yesterday night."

"What? I told you something?" Kavya's face suddenly turned pale.

"Yeah. Everything that happened after you heard Riya crying, all the family drama, how you chose your parents over me, dad's business loss, heart attack and how Riya and Aditya came to the rescue."

"Oh my God! When did I tell you all this?"

"At night. You were talking in your sleep. You called my name, you held my hands, and told me everything."

Kavya was mortified. Her hands grew cold. She wanted to take everything back. She shouldn't have said all that. She felt embarrassed about her confession, knowing now that Rehan had probably moved on with someone named Tulika. She felt like an idiot.

"It's okay. You wanted to spit it out, so you did. And it's not just you, my feelings for you are not gone either," Rehan said, as he put his hands on hers and looked in to her eyes.

Kavya sat there for a moment. Then, she looked at Rehan and asked, "Who is Tulika, Rehan?"

Rehan was stumped by this question. He didn't know what had made her ask that question. His face lost its glow.

"What?" he asked. He didn't know how to respond.

"I saw the other room. Does she live with you here? Is she your girlfriend, Rehan?" Her voice trembled a bit.

Rehan had not expected Kavya to find about this on her own. He was now at a loss of words. He said, "I was going to tell you about this. Tulika and I are good friends and we share this flat. She is just a friend. That's it. Nothing more."

Kavya felt uncomfortable. Rehan's explanation was starting to annoy her. She felt like a loser. No one would feel comfortable on hearing about a counterpart in their lover's life.

When Rehan tried to explain, she interrupted him: "I think I should go now. Thanks for letting me stay here for the night, Rehan."

"Kavya, listen! There is nothing like what you are thinking."

Kavya took her bag and stormed out of the room. She put on her shoes and walked out of the flat. Rehan was left standing in the living room, feeling bewildered.

He went to his room, grabbed his phone and followed Kavya in the lift. Kavya had already walked out of the apartment building. A few moments later, Rehan followed her onto the road. He saw Kavya walking down the road, and called after her. She didn't listen. Rehan saw her talking to a taxi driver, so he started running towards her as fast as he could.

"Kavya, wait…" he shouted.

He followed her through the streets. As he reached the crossroads, a car appeared out of nowhere and hit Rehan. A sudden 'thump' and the screech of tires made every vehicle stop. Kavya heard the noise and looked back—she saw Rehan slide down and hit the pavement. Blood poured from his head.

Kavya got out of the taxi and ran to him. She kneeled beside him and cradled his head. "Rehan! Rehan!" she called out to him again and again. Tears rolled down her cheeks and landed on his face. Rehan had passed out.

Someone from the crowd called an ambulance. Kavya went with Rehan to the hospital. On the way, she held Rehan's head close to her heart. She prayed to God to make things alright. She continuously checked his heartbeat. Whether it was her love or the fear of losing Rehan again, she wasn't sure. Throughout the way she kept looking at the road, hoping that the hospital would appear soon. Every passing second felt like an hour to her.

They reached the hospital. Rehan was admitted in the emergency wing. The nurse handed Rehan's phone and wallet to Kavya. She waited outside while they took Rehan into the operation theater. Kavya sat outside. She was still sobbing. She closed her eyes and prayed to god. She blamed herself for the accident. If she hadn't rushed out of the flat, Rehan wouldn't have followed and none of this would have happened. She cried.

"Ma'am, could you please fill this form?" she heard a nurse speaking to her.

Kavya took the form and started to fill it. Name, age, address and phone number…. Suddenly, there came a field where her hands started to shake: 'Relationship with the patient.' She wrote her name down, and put down 'Friend.' She couldn't find any other appropriate word.

While Kavya was filling the form, Rehan's phone rang. It was Tulika. Kavya wasn't sure whether to pick it up or not. As Rehan's friend, though, Tulika should know about what had happened. So, Kavya finally picked up the phone.

Chapter 8
Tulika

"Helllloooow!" Tulika said in a sing-song tone.

"Hi," Kavya replied.

Tulika hadn't expected a girl to answer Rehan's phone. She checked the number again to confirm that she had dialed the correct number.

"Who's this?" Tulika asked politely.

"I'm Kavya. Rehan's friend."

"Where's Rehan?"

"Listen, Tulika. You need to know something." She paused. "Actually, Rehan is in the hospital."

"What?" Tulika screamed. "What happened?"

"He had an accident. He's now in the Operation Theatre."

Tulika was stunned. She didn't say anything. She just breathed heavily.

"Hello…Tulika…? You there? Tulika? Where are you? If you are listening, come to Hiranandani Hospital."

Tulika was about to board a plane back to Mumbai. Her smile faded away. She had something in her hand—a ring.

What was Rehan to her? Just a roommate, or more than that? Why was she feeling so upset?

Unlike Rehan and Kavya, Tulika was born with a silver spoon. She was the only heir to Lalit Mahajan's property, which was worth several crores. She was blessed with beauty as well. However, no one's life is perfect—neither was Tulika's. Despite all the money and glamour around her, Tulika never had peace of mind since childhood.

When she was seven, she saw her mom and dad fight every day. They would scream and curse at each other and what not. This was beyond the understanding of a seven-year-old. What her childish mind interpreted was that she should never love or marry anyone—otherwise, she would end up just like her parents. That idea persisted for years.

What she didn't know was her parents had had a love marriage. Be it love or arranged, when things don't work out the way they were supposed to, the couple start to drift apart. The same had happened with her parents.

Everyday, Tulika would return from school and listen to her mom bitching about her father to someone on the phone. She would stand at the door, waiting for her mom to put down the phone and come play with her. She would wait until she grew tired. Then, she would go to her room and play with her toys—alone.

Most kids spend their childhood listening to stories, watching cartoons or talking about ghosts and goblins. Tulika had nothing but loneliness. She had to eat alone at the gigantic dining table. Sometimes, she felt that her parents had forgotten about her after giving birth to her. Whom could she have complained to? Her mom was mostly busy on phone. Her dad would come back late, and he was usually tired. When she went up to him, he would have fallen asleep. She began to accept life for how it was and stopped complaining. She embraced loneliness, for it was her only constant.

She had no 'normal' days till she was sixteen. First the nanny, and then the maid—they were the only ones Tulika was ever close to at home. It didn't matter how much fun she had at school—when she went back home, she felt alone and depressed. She would lock herself in her room for hours and listen to loud music just to keep herself distracted from her parents' drama.

When she grew tired of it, she started to stay at her friend's places.

She had many friends at school—all of them were rich, spoiled brats. Tulika spent most of her time with them. She rarely went to her own house. When she did, she locked herself in her room.

Eventually, things became worse and her parents separated. Her mom moved to Dehradun, to Tulika's grandma's place. Before she moved, she asked Tulika to come with her but the girl decided to stay in Udaipur. Not because she loved her dad, but because she didn't want to leave her friends.

After the separation, her dad paid more attention to the business and to her. She was all he had left. One day, he sat down with Tulika and talked about all the disputes he had had with her mother. He explained how relationships don't work out if you don't nourish them from time to time. He took her out for dinner frequently, and they had a good time. Tulika and her dad bonded really well. However, though she enjoyed her dad's company, it was too late. Not too late for accepting the love and affection his father was showering upon her, but too late to gain faith in love.

Being a businessman, her dad couldn't afford much time for her. So, Tulika partied all the time with her friends. That was her only way of keeping herself occupied and happy. Just like all of her rich friends, she started smoking and drinking from an early age. She roamed around day and night with them. She bunked classes to watch movies, to shop or hang out at some bar.

She had her first tattoo when she was 17—of a camera with feathers flying around it. She had developed an interest in photography, so she joined a club the same year. She went on trips with the club and practiced photography. Like cigarettes and alcohol, photography became her addiction. She frequently went on trips with the club members. After a year, she dropped out of college so that she could pursue photography full-time. Tulika's dad never stopped her from doing anything she liked. He knew that he had destroyed her childhood—and he didn't want to make it worse by interfering in her adulthood. He kept an eye on her, though, about where she was going and what she was doing.

Tulika's life was going well. She was free as a bird. She had a father who would throw money at anything she pointed to, so she didn't find it hard to keep herself happy. In her early twenties, she started covering wedding events with some of her colleagues from the club. Not that she lived for the money she got from the gigs, but it felt good to travel across India, meet new people and capture their happy moments.

One year later, the club offered her a solo gig. She was very happy as she had always wanted that. It was a wedding in West Bengal. Tulika had always wanted to travel to the east of India—and she finally got a chance.

When the day arrived, she flew to West Bengal. She was excited, and looked forward to getting started. She reached there a day earlier, to look at the place and set up her frames for the next two days. It was a huge palace—she admired the grandness and beauty of it. She met the bride and groom. They were warm hosts, and had arranged for a room for her.

The next day, Tulika put on a traditional outfit and started shooting the rituals. She didn't have any idea about the regional marriage rituals in the east. Not only did she click many pictures, but she learned many things about Bengalis. Their food, culture, language and world-famous roshogulla.

She was busy all day, capturing every moment of the event. The happy people, the *mehendi*, dance and everything. While she was on the first floor, setting her tripod for a top angle shot, she saw a handsome guy with a beautiful girl entering the gate. She saw the bride running up to that girl and hugging her. She looked at the guy, just for a moment. His smile was charming. She looked away and continued with her tripod. While she was fitting the camera, she looked at him again out of the corner of her eye. It was a strange feeling. She had never felt such a thing before.

The wedding day arrived. Tulika knew it was going to be a busy day for her. She had to be up and about continuously, until the marriage rituals ended. She had charged the batteries and emptied the SD cards. She wore a long white *kurta* and a blue *salwar*. She was ready with her camera to start rolling. When she was taking a wide-angle shot of the *mandap* with the background she saw the same guy she had seen the day before; he was coming down the stairs. He looked cute in a blue *kurta* and white pajama. She looked at him for a second and then went back to her work.

Sometime later, while she was checking out the pictures, she heard a voice from behind. It was a manly yet charming voice. She turned around. It was the same guy. He stood in front of her with a smile on his face. Tulika smiled back.

"So, you are here to cover the wedding?" he asked.

"Yeah."

"Nice camera."

"Thanks."

"I'm Rehan." The guy extended his hand.

"Hi. I'm Tulika." She shook his hand.

"So, you are from the bride's side?" she asked.

"Technically, no. I'm the friend of the bride's sister."

"That puts you on the bride's side."

"Ha-ha. I guess."

They both chuckled.

"I am also a photographer. Not a professional though but I run my club at college. I like taking pictures," Rehan said.

"Oh nice. That's good. Didn't you bring your camera along?"

"I just had an early session with the bride and the groom. Now, I'll enjoy the wedding," he said as he made a funny face.

"Ha-ha. Okay."

"So, where are you from?"

"I stay in Mumbai, but I belong to Udaipur."

"Great."

"And you?"

"Well, I stay in Indore. I study there. But I am from Bhubaneswar"

"Indore? Wow. One of my cousins stays there."

"Yeah?"

"Which college are you in?" she asked.

"IIT Indore."

"IIT! Wow. Geek!" she said as she grinned at him.

"Ha-ha. No. I'm anything but a geek."

They both laughed. Rehan asked her whether she was freelancing or if she belonged to a group. She told him about her group. Rehan expressed his interest in being a professional photographer, so Tulika passed him her card—in case he needed any help.

Tulika had to get back to work, so Rehan took off from there. She ran the conversation a couple of times in her mind. She liked Rehan. The way he talked, and the passion in his voice. Later, when it rained at the wedding, Tulika ran to take shelter, when she saw Rehan standing alongside with the girl he had come with. The view looked beautiful from where she was standing. She took a picture of Rehan with the girl.

Soon after, the rain ended and so did the wedding. While Tulika was wrapping up her gadgets to take leave from the hosts, she searched for Rehan but he was not to be seen. That was the first time she had missed someone, even if it was for just a second.

She went back to Mumbai. After that wedding, she got three more wedding offers in the same month—two in south India and one in Delhi.

~Two Months Later

Given her recent successful gigs, Tulika threw a party for her colleagues. In Mumbai, parties go on till morning. Tulika was four shots down when she heard her phone beep. It was three-thirty in the morning. She got a text from an unknown number. It read: *Hey. Remember? Rehan, The guy from IIT, we met in West Bengal two months back, in a wedding, you gave me your card. I need your help.*

Tulika didn't remember at first, maybe because she was drunk, but she figured it out. She replied to him and asked him to call her the next day.

Tulika was glad that Rehan had texted her. She smiled. She had a couple more shots.

The next afternoon, she got a call. She picked up the call; it was quiet for a few seconds. Then, a voice came from the other side.

"Hi."

"Hello?" Tulika replied a bit apprehensively. "Who's this?"

"Rehan! I texted you in the morning, at four… you were at a party."

"Oh yeah! Hi Rehan. What's up?"

"How was the party last night?"

"It was good."

"Nice."

"So tell me…"

"I saw all your clicks on Facebook. They are beautiful. You are really talented."

"Thanks."

"I loved the rain pictures. Specially the one you had taken at that wedding—of me and my friend."

"Oh yeah. That one. I also love that picture. It reminds me of how I used to get drenched in the rain," she said. She paused and then continued, "Anyway, you didn't tell me what help you wanted."

"So I…uh…know this is kind of awkward but I needed a gig and I remembered that we had talked about it that day. So, as I was reaching out to people for help, I thought, why not call someone I know?"

"A gig? What happened to your studies?" Tulika was a little shocked. She didn't understand why an IIT student would need a gig. She was confused.

"Urm…I dropped out."

"Really?"

"Yeah."

It seemed familiar to her, as she had also dropped out of college. She said, "That's cool."

"So, would you be able to get me one?" he asked.

"Well…I might have something but let me check with my team first. I'll get back to you. Okay?"

"Yeah. Sure."

He sounded serious, and she wanted to help him. So, she called one of her senior team members. She said that she had a friend who was a good photographer and needed a job badly. Unfortunately, there was no vacancy—all events were already assigned. Tulika was disappointed. She really wanted to help Rehan. She had a soft spot for him, although she didn't know why. She asked her senior if she could pass on one of her assignments to Rehan. The senior didn't seem convinced about a new guy replacing a professional. However, Tulika convinced him somehow and got Rehan the job.

Then, she called Rehan.

"Congratulations! I got you a job," she said.

"Really? Thank you so much, Tulika!" Rehan seemed very excited.

"Don't thank me yet. You will have to come to Mumbai first. My team wants to meet you before they hand over the assignment."

"Okay, no problem. I'll be there."

"You have to be here by this weekend. Can you make it?"

"Yeah, I will be there."

"Perfect."

She could hear Rehan jumping on the other side of the phone. She could feel his joy.

She didn't know why she had sacrificed her job for a total stranger—but it felt like the right thing to do.

~Thursday

Tulika was excited about meeting Rehan. She left her flat earlier than usual that day. She was on her way to the office when she got a call from Rehan. He was in a taxi, heading to the address that she had sent him earlier. She told him to let her know if he reached before her so that she could arrange things for him. Tulika sped up her scooter. In fifteen minutes, she reached the office and met Rehan. Tulika introduced Rehan to everyone at work, and later took him to the studio where she taught him a few basic camera tricks. To her surprise, Rehan knew them all. She was impressed by his talent. The next day, Rehan had to leave for the event. Tulika joined him, to guide him if needed. However, he managed everything really well. She sat there and watched him working with a lot of passion. She admired his eagerness to work. The event went well, and Rehan completed his first gig successfully. Tulika was happy for him.

Tulika lived in a big two-bedroom flat. Her dad had bought it for her. *Little perks of having a rich father.* She used to throw parties every Friday night at her place and invite her friends. She didn't have many friends in Mumbai. In fact, she didn't have any friends in Mumbai, except the ones she met at discos or pubs. This time, she invited Rehan, too.

Rehan came. He sat in a corner, drank a beer. Tulika was busy dancing with her friends. She saw Rehan sitting silently and sipping beer. She went to him and invited him to dance with her. Rehan wasn't an outgoing person, so he respectfully desisted. She didn't force him either. She sat there with him, and they both talked. It didn't last long, as she ran out of topics. And to her bad luck, Rehan wasn't much of a talker. Soon, she joined her friends on the dance floor. Rehan stayed for a bit longer and then left. After that, Tulika called Rehan every Friday.

Three years passed. Things were going good. One day, Tulika called Rehan to her place. She was upset. Rehan showed up immediately. Tulika's face was streaked with tears; her eyes were moist. After they sat on the couch, Tulika turned towards him and asked, "Do I look like a slut?"

Rehan was shocked, yet he remained silent.

"Tell me Rehan, do you also think of me as a fucking slut?" Her tone grew louder.

"What? Why are you asking me this? What happened?" Rehan asked. He seemed concerned.

"An hour earlier, one guy came here. I met him at a pub last week and gave him my number. He called me and asked if he could drop by. I said 'yes.' He came and started flirting with me. It was okay until he put his hands on my hips. I pushed him. He still didn't get his hands off. I pushed him harder this time, got up from the sofa and asked him to leave. He got up and left, but he called me a slut before leaving, and asked me why I gave him my number if I didn't want to sleep with him." She took a deep breath and continued, "Rehan, I know I am a fun-loving girl. I am very broad-minded. I drink, I smoke. But that doesn't make me a slut, does it? Do you also think of me as a slut?"

"No. Not at all," Rehan said as he opened his arms to hug Tulika.

Tulika hugged him.

"For all these years I've known you, I have always had only two things for you: admiration and respect. The way you live your life makes me feel envious and I wish I could live like that. But the truth is, I can't. In fact, very few people can. You are independent, confident and talented. All I see in you is a winner. A winner at life. And winners should never listen to douchebags," Rehan comforted her.

To hear such wonderful words from a person you like drives away all kinds of worries and pain. Tulika felt a strange sense of belongingness with Rehan. She suddenly felt an urge to tell him about her past.

He nodded as he listened, and kept her warm in his arms. He kept her wrapped inside a protective bubble while she told him her story.

Then, there came a moment of silence. Tulika had stopped talking. She felt secure in Rehan's arms. She didn't want to let him go that night, so she stayed right there in his arms.

"Are you okay?" Rehan asked.

"Yeah."

She looked into his eyes—they were innocent and comforting. She lifted her chin. Her breath landed on Rehan's lips. Their lips were just a few centimeters away from each other. Rehan leaned towards Tulika; with a final push, Tulika reached his lips. They kissed. She hugged him tight. He hugged her, too. Soon they moved into the bedroom.

That night, Tulika felt peace for the very first time in her life. She was wrapped in Rehan's arms, and rested on his chest. She felt complete. She felt amazing. Outside, the stars twinkled, as if they were happy for her. She could hear symphonies playing inside her mind. She was happy. Very happy.

The next morning, she woke up early. She picked up her clothes and went inside the bathroom to change.

Sometime later, Rehan woke up. Tulika offered him some coffee. He smiled.

"I had a great time last night," she said.

"Me too." Rehan said.

"So what's your plan for today?"

"Nothing. I am flat-hunting."

"You already have a place, right?"

"Yes. But the landlord is too strict about timings. The room is good but that guy is so irritating. So, I'm looking for another room."

"Okay."

Suddenly an idea struck her. "Hey, why don't you move in with me? Anyway, this is a big place for just one person. Also, with you being here, I won't feel lonely—so no more stupid parties."

"Here?"

"Yeah."

"Well..." Rehan sounded awkward.

"What?"

"Are you sure?"

"Yeah. You can call off your flat-hunting program," she said in a childish yet bossy way, as she got up and walked to the kitchen.

"Okay," he said and smiled.

The next day, Rehan moved in with Tulika. She was really happy. Days passed. Their friendship grew stronger. Apart from work, they spent a lot of time together. Tulika stopped going to the pubs and partying at home. She began to change from being a spoiled person to a responsible one.

Tulika liked Rehan a lot. She admired his passion, his sincerity and truthfulness. Her feelings for Rehan came into the picture when he had hugged her that night. She had fallen for the love she had so desperately dodged throughout her life. She enjoyed Rehan's company very much. They ate, played together, watched movies and went out together. But after that night, they did not sleep together.

Tulika thought that was a night of weakness. She was vulnerable and couldn't stop herself. She didn't want to make it a casual friendship by bringing in sex. She wanted it to be meaningful. Now that two years had passed, she wanted to take the next step. She knew that she loved Rehan and she wanted to ask him the same. She hoped it would turn out well, so she decided to talk to her dad about it first.

One day, she made an excuse of work and went to Udaipur to meet her dad. *The same day Rehan met Kavya at the café.*

It had been a long time since she had met her dad. She hugged him and told him how happy she was with her life. Her dad was surprised to see her full of life. They went out for dinner that night; there, Tulika told him about Rehan. "Dad, I want to tell you something. It's about a man I love. I know this sounds weird, me talking about love and all. But life tricked me into it. I didn't choose this—destiny chose it for me. I have never thought of being with someone except myself but, as it turned out, I was wrong.

"I had no idea that he would come into my life and make it so much beautiful. His name is Rehan. I met him five years ago. You will freak out if you hear that he is a dropout from IIT. He wanted to have a career in photography and he needed my help. I gave him an opportunity and he made it to the peak. He's been a very good friend of mine since that day. We are living together in my flat for last two years. We share a very good understanding. He cares for me and looks out for me. I think he is the one. You know what…I could have said it to him right away but I wanted to tell you first. So…" Tulika paused and looked at her dad.

Her dad smiled. He cupped her cheeks with his palm and kissed her forehead. "Tulika, baby, the thing which your mom and I had was love. It was so beautiful at first and we were so happy. But we were not able to take care of it that well. When you get love, you should cherish it and protect it. But we didn't. Eventually, things started to fall out. She was busy with her life and I was busy with my business. Then, you were born.

"Have you ever wondered about you being our only child? Well that was because we started drifting apart from each other. We were together just for the society and our relatives. But it didn't go well, as you know. We had our problems but we both loved you so much. You have to understand the fact that you are neither of your parents. You are you, the girl who doesn't care for the society, the girl who follows her dream, the girl who loves the way she is. I actually feel honored that you told me about it. It seems that you have found love, sweetheart.

Just keep it safe, and protect it. You will be happy. I promise," her dad said.

Tulika had not seen this side of her dad before. She admired him even more after this. She smiled and thanked her dad. The next day she went to a jewelry shop and bought a ring. She had decided that, if Rehan were on the same page as her, then she would ask him to marry her.

That night, she called Rehan. He was at a party with some friend. She was feeling restless about the next day, when she would propose to him.

The next morning, she called Rehan but he didn't pick up. She called him many times but he didn't pick up. She was a little worried; the fact that she was going to propose to him was keeping her on edge. She guessed that Rehan was sleeping, so she decided to call him later. She called him from the airport. This time, someone answered—a feminine voice came from the other side. The girl who spoke said that her name was Kavya, and that Rehan had had an accident.

Chapter 9

The Hospital

20 January 2016

Kavya was sitting outside the operation theater. She was constantly looking at the little red light, hoping that it would be turned off soon. She felt guilty for everything that had happened. Tears rolled down from her eyes.

Her legs had become numb; her hands were lying on her thighs, lifeless. Earlier, she had overheard the doctor talking to the nurse about "internal bleeding," "cerebral damage," and "multiple fractures"—which scared her terribly. She prayed to God to make everything alright. That was all she could do.

She thought that nothing would have happened if she had said everything to Rehan at the pub itself. Neither would she have gotten drunk nor would Rehan have brought her back to his room. Above all, she shouldn't have reacted the way she did at Rehan's apartment. Rehan had all the rights to move on—five years was a long time after all. So what if he didn't tell her anything about the other girl? She had no right to feel upset about it, given what she had done to Rehan in the past. She felt terrible. The whirl of guilt dragged her down.

The red light finally went off after an hour. Kavya quickly grabbed her bag and walked to the door. She was restless and eagerly waited for someone to open the door and come out. Her palms were sweaty. She mumbled, "Please God, he should be okay, he should be okay. Please…"

The doctor opened the door.

"How is he? Is he alright? Is everything okay?" she asked the doctor.

"Yes. He is okay. There was only some external damage. Nothing internal, as we had feared. You can relax. He is out of danger now," the doctor said.

"Thank god."

"He is still unconscious, so someone needs to stay with him for the next 24 hours."

"Yeah. I will be here until he wakes up."

"That's good."

"Thank you, doctor," Kavya sighed with relief. She felt a little relaxed. She looked into the cabin, through the small glass pane on the door. She saw the nurse injecting a saline needle into his wrist. She thanked God for making everything alright. She stood there until the nurses came out. She asked one of the nurses if she could go inside.

"Not Now. Once he is shifted to the private ward you can see him," said the nurse.

"When will that happen?" Kavya asked.

"We'll let you know," the nurse replied.

"Okay."

Kavya waited outside.

A few hours later, they shifted him to a ward.

Kavya slowly opened the door. She stood beside Rehan and whispered, "I'm sorry." Though he couldn't hear her, she kept saying, "I'm sorry." There had never as much love in her eyes for Rehan before. Just then, Rehan's phone rang. It was Tulika again. Kavya was asked to go out to take the call.

"Hello," Tulika said.

"Hi Tulika, where are you?" Kavya asked.

"How is Rehan? Is he okay?" Tulika stuttered.

"Yes. He is out of danger now. He's resting. Where are you?"

"I'm in Udaipur. My last flight just got cancelled. The next flight is in the evening. I will be there by six. Please take care of him."

"Yeah. I will be here till you get here."

Kavya remembered the last conversation she had had with Rehan. He had said that Tulika was just a good friend but the pain in Tulika's voice when she asked about Rehan gave Kavya a different vibe. She felt a sense of uneasiness. She unlocked Rehan's phone (there was no password), and checked some of his pictures. Tulika and Rehan seemed happy in the photos—even happier than how Rehan and she had been. She felt this was not a place for her to take. The void had been filled. She had lost Rehan due to her stupidity. She pulled her hand away from Rehan's. She reached into her bag and pulled out her journal. She knew that this might be her last meeting with Rehan, so she wanted to tell him everything. Though Rehan was unconscious, she read out everything she had written over the years. She began with their first meeting.

Page after page, she kept reading. She relived the experiences. Suddenly, her eyes caught a movement. Rehan's fingers were moving. She thought he would wake up. She kept the diary, half-open, on the table, and spoke to him softly. His fingers were still moving. She rushed to the nurse and told her about it. The nurse called the doctor and they both checked on whether Rehan was coming back to his senses. However, the doctor dismissed the fact that he was waking up. He said that it was a mild muscle reflex, but added that that was a good sign and that Rehan may recover sooner than they predicted. Kavya breathed easy. After they left, Kavya slowly brushed Rehan's hair with her fingers. She looked at him and said, "Rehan, it is better that you wake up after I'm gone from here," she said. She felt a bit dizzy, as she hadn't eaten anything all day. She wanted to rinse her face and get some coffee. She quickly grabbed her bag and went out.

While picking up the coffee from the vending machine, she saw the time. It was thirty past six in the evening. Tulika would be reaching soon. She sat on the bench and sipped the coffee. Memories haunted her. She put the coffee aside and went to the restroom to wash her face. She looked at herself in the mirror.

"You are doing the right thing," the reflection said.

"That's what you said five years ago. Remember?" Kavya argued.

"Well, tell me, did you have any other choice then. Did you know that, eventually, your dad would turn around and approve of your sister's marriage?"

"No."

"Now you have two people in front of you. Their relationship is shaping up and, who knows, they might end up being together. Would you come in their way and ruin that?"

"No"

"Then say goodbye to Rehan and leave. Let's face it—you and Rehan are not destined to be together. So, forget it and start a new life."

'Everything the reflection said is true,' Kavya thought. She made up her mind. She washed her face and walked to the cabin to say goodbye to Rehan. When she reached, she saw a lady already sitting beside Rehan and holding his hands. She could have gone inside and discovered who the lady was herself but she didn't. She suspected that it was Tulika and she didn't want to face her, as she wasn't comfortable doing so. She went to the reception to check—she got to know that the lady inside was indeed Tulika. She walked to the door again to see them together. She saw Tulika sitting close to Rehan and gently stroking his hair. She didn't want to go inside and interrupt them, so she said goodbye to Rehan right there. "See you someday, Rehan. Be happy. Get well soon." She walked away. She was walking away from Rehan once again.

She stepped out of the hospital. She remembered that she had left her car at the pub, so she took a cab to the pub. On the way, she thought about how awkward it would be to bump into each other in future. So, she decided to move to another city. On the way, she emailed her boss and requested him to transfer her to the Hyderabad office. Even before she reached the pub, she had gotten a reply back from her boss—he was more than delighted to send her to the Hyderabad office, for an even bigger role.

At the hospital, Rehan was still unconscious. Tulika sat beside him, feeling that she should have never left him. She looked out for Kavya, who hadn't come in since she had arrived. When she enquired about it at the reception, she was told that Kavya had left just five minutes after she had arrived. She thought it was weird, but she didn't think of it as a big deal. She went into the cabin and sat there. A few minutes later, the nurse went in to change the saline. "You are not the same girl who brought him here, are you?" the nurse asked Tulika.

"Urm...no. I just got here now," Tulika replied.

"You are also a friend?"

"Yes. How did it happen, sister? Did the other girl tell anything about it?" she asked.

"It was a car accident. He was walking on the road and suddenly got hit by a car."

"Okay."

The nurse changed the saline and walked away. Tulika looked at Rehan. She remembered how happy she had been about coming back to Mumbai, to surprise him. She took out the ring and looked at it. She thought she would wait for Rehan to recover fully, and then tell him about it. She put the ring back in her purse and walked to the window. She saw the skyline of concrete pillars, twinkling in the distance. She closed her eyes. Just then, she heard her phone ring. Her dad was calling. She picked up.

"Hey. When did you reach?" her dad asked.

"Hey dad. My morning flight was cancelled so I had to board in the afternoon."

"So, did you talk to Rehan?"

"Dad, Rehan is in hospital."

"What happened?"

"He met an accident."

"Is he okay?"

"Everything is alright now. He is resting and I'm with him."

"Sweetheart, do you want me to come down?"

"No dad. It's okay. I can handle this."

"Take care of him, little girl. Call me if you need anything."

"Yeah. Thanks dad. Bye."

She hung up and turned around. She wished Rehan would recover soon. She was walking to the sofa when her eye caught something on the table.

Chapter 10

The Gift

Present

~December 2018, Bhubaneswar

I am going to attend a marriage reception. It is a beautiful afternoon. I am driving my car through the roads of Bhubaneswar, basking in the winter air. The sun is ready to set behind the west horizon; an orange splashed all over the western sky. The view looks serene.

I have been here before, twice. Both times for work. I find this city very clean and refreshing. I like their language—it's sweet. You feel a strange sense of belonging while talking to the people here. Few of my friends stay here; they are warm hosts. Another thing that I like about Odia people is their delicious food—I could eat it all day.

The cold wind ruffles my hair; my body shivers. I put the roof back on and turn on the heater. It is really cold outside; my body isn't used to this kind of weather. I've been living in Goa for the last seven years, so I'm used to coastal climate—not so cold and not so hot.

A few minutes later, I check the map. It shows thirty more minutes to the destination. I sit back and drive along with the traffic. The traffic is moving very slowly. I take a look at the gift on the left seat—it is packed with colorful glittery paper. It looks beautiful. I admire my girl's decorating sense. She is a pro. Actually, it is her friend's marriage reception that I'm going to attend. She has also attached a letter, which is sealed inside an envelope.

The traffic clears. I drive another ten minutes before I hit another block. The roads are very busy as it is evening time. People are returning from work; students are going back from schools and colleges. I pick the left lane. I look to the left and see a temple. A bunch of people dressed in orange are lighting *diyas* and playing a metal instrument. I love the fact that people here are very religious. The ambience is pious. I have never felt such positive energy inside me. The sun has set, and it is getting darker now. It is six-thirty already. The map says I have twenty more minutes to go.

After half an hour, I reach the venue—The Mayfair Lagoon. I can see the grand white building through the narrow gaps between the trees. I see magnificent lighting throughout the road. It looks like a pathway to heaven. There are lots of cars in front of me, crawling like tortoises.

I park my car near a statue of Lord Krishna and Arjun on a chariot. If you have seen any documentary on Bhubaneswar, you would have seen this wonderful statue standing near the entrance of the hotel. It is a trademark scene from the Mahabharata.

I come out of my car with the gift and letter in my hand. I quickly take a picture of the statue.

I walk to the entrance gate. It is huge, and the floral decoration on it looks rich and beautiful. Men dressed in sherwanis and women dressed in saris are standing at the gate and welcoming the guests. Most of the people are wearing ethnic clothes. I am wearing a formal white shirt, a maroon blazer and a pair of faded blue jeans. I feel a bit out of place. Anyway, people at the entrance welcome me with wide smiles and a warm "Namaste." I walk in. I see a long red carpet; people are walking in front of me. I see the couple standing at the end of the carpet, under a humungous canopy. All the jewels and glittery decorations are flashing.

I walk towards the couple. I walk straight to the canopy. I see the happy couple shaking hands with their friends and family and taking pictures. I remember my girlfriend's words. She said, "They are going to be the happiest couple in the world." Now, I can see why. I reach the stage. I take a few steps towards the couple when Rehan, the groom, smiles at me. He is wearing a red *sherwani*, with a *sehra* on his head. His beard is a bit longer than in his old pictures. He looks handsome. I am not sure if he recognizes me or not. We haven't actually met before. I stretch out my hand for a handshake. He shakes my hand, thanks me for coming and introduces me to his wife. Then, he walks to a group of people who seem to his friends.

She looks very beautiful in her bridal attire. She is, no doubt, the most beautiful woman there today. I see her eyes—they are shining like diamonds. She smiles when Rehan glances at her from a distance. I walk to her side.

"You look beautiful," I say to her.

"Thanks," she replies.

She thinks of me as Rehan's friend, but the truth is that I'm neither his friend nor hers. I am here to deliver a gift. She takes it from me with a smile on her face, and stretches her arm to keep it on the gifts table. Rehan is busy talking to his friends. I take this opportunity to talk to her.

"Don't you want to know who it is from?" I ask.

She looks at me strangely. She seems confused. She holds the gift while looking at me with a questioning stare. She smiles awkwardly as she reads the sticker on the cover.

From Tulika.

She is shocked. Her eyes become big and her smile seems uncertain. She looks at me. I see questions arising in her eyes. The next moment, she rips apart the wrapping and finds a diary inside it. She is dumbstruck, as she seems to have recognized it.

I know that she is trying to connect the dots, but she doesn't have all the dots. Not yet.

I give her the letter. "Read it," I tell her.

She quickly opens the envelope and reads the letter.

Hi Kavya. First of all, congratulations to Rehan and you. I'm sorry I couldn't make it to your wedding though I knew about it. Also, sorry for not showing up today as well. We have never met each other, and I would like to keep it this way. I know you have a lot of questions in your mind now... believe me, I had more that day...

~ Two Years Ago, Hiranandani Hospital, Mumbai

"Take care of him, little girl. Call me if you need anything."

"Yeah. Thanks dad. Bye," Tulika said.

She hung up and turned around to look at Rehan. The sight of Rehan covered in bandages was very hard to look at. She leaned against the wall and closed her eyes in remorse. Loneliness usually takes one into a realm of dark emotions. Guilt is one of them. As Tulika was alone at that time, she started to think that everything was her fault. She shouldn't have left Rehan in the first place. She was walking to the sofa when her eye caught something on the table.

There was a diary, half-open, sitting on the table. It seemed like someone's journal, given the way it was painted with colors and decorated with stickers. She wasn't sure if she should read it or not. Reading someone else's journal isn't quite a good idea, but she felt a strange urge to look at it. She took the journal and sat on the sofa.

"Is it Kavya's? Did she forget it here? Should I read it?" she asked herself. Though she had the journal in her hand she wasn't fully sure about whether she should open it. Finally, not being able to fight her compulsion, she turned over the cover. The inside page read: *Kavya Kapoor*. She promptly turned over the first page and scanned it—there was no mention of Rehan. She turned over the next page. She had decided not to read anything that didn't mention Rehan.

After a few pages, she finally found Rehan's name. The date on the page was September 27, 2010.

27.09.10

Today was different. I met Rehan. We had tea in the canteen. He is funny and sweet. He has a way of talking. I must say I am impressed. I couldn't stop thinking about him all day. I want to meet him again but I can't be too hasty about it. Let him ask me out.

Waiting...

Hah! This feels good.

I'm dropping him a goodnight message.

This stirred something inside Tulika. She wanted to know more. Rehan had never mentioned this girl to her before, which made her even more curious. She turned the next page. Now, she didn't skip a single word.

28.09.10

We met again today. He called me to the canteen. We talked for a while. He is so charming. He asked me for a movie this Friday. I think I'll go.

30.09.10

It was a great day. We went to the movies and had dinner. I enjoyed it.

On the ride back to the campus, a strange thing happened. We were in the cab and talking, when he suddenly placed his hands on mine. It was sudden but very gentle. I felt awkward but I didn't want to slip away my hands from him.

It's only three days! What is happening?

14.10.10

He sat with me in the college bus. Everybody from my class was staring at us but he was casual. We talked all the way to the campus. I laughed so hard.

He called me for a walk after dinner. While we were walking, he touched my hands again. This time it didn't feel so awkward. How does he do it so gently? Many guys had hit on me before. Their attempts were mostly dumb and cheap but Rehan is different. I don't even feel like he's making a move. He makes it so smooth. Maybe he is genuinely sweet.

Let's give it some time.

23.10.10

At the airport. Going home for seven days. Rehan drove me to the airport. I am going to miss him. I wish the seven days would pass quickly.

25.11.10

Tomorrow is physics exam. I hate this subject. I wasn't able to solve the questions. I was freaking out. I told Rehan about it. He called me to the canteen. We sat there. We had coffee. He told me about some of his craziest exam preparation experiences and that cheered me up. I was laughing. Later, when I came back to the room, I felt fresh. Thanks Rehan!

16.12.10

Rehan and I had the longest conversation on the phone today. I was missing him and so was he, I guess. He is in Bhubaneswar and I'm in Chandigarh. We are thousands of miles apart but when we talk on the phone I feel he's just beside me. Fifteen more days to go. I can't wait to see him again.

Tulika continued reading. She didn't find anything but Kavya and Rehan in the pages. One page after another, she witnessed their closeness. She learned about their friendship and how it became stronger with every passing day. Kavya had written of her time with Rehan. Their movie and dinner dates, evening walks and canteen meetings. Tulika was lost in their story. She also felt jealous.

7.03.2011

It was the last day of our college festival. KK came for the concert. I love his songs. He sings so effortlessly. I was standing with Rehan, holding his hands. When KK started 'Mera pehla pehla pyar,' I looked at Rehan. He looked at me too. He held me tight in his arms. I felt safe and warm. I closed my eyes and rested on his shoulders.

On the way back to the campus, in the bus, we kissed. It was long. He kisses so passionately. I didn't want to let go but I had to. I was relieved that no one in the bus saw us.

We've not told each other anything about our feelings yet. I don't know when that is going to happen.

A chill ran down Tulika's spine. She felt discomfited. She didn't know how to react to it, even though it was in the past. She wanted to know more. She vigorously turned the pages just to witness what happened later. She found a lot of hugging, kissing and being with each other, until she reached…

5.11.2011

Yesssssssss! I am going to Riya's marriage. I can't believe it. I had nearly lost all hopes of attending her wedding, thanks to my dad. But then, Rehan came in like a ray of hope. He is taking me to the marriage. He cares so much for me. The final exams are coming, yet he doesn't care about it. I think the time has come. I should tell him about my feelings. It's been more than a year now.

6.11.2011

My dad hates Riya because she is having an inter-caste marriage. The way he was talking to her over the phone…no one talks to their daughter like that. I don't want my dad to hate me like that. I don't want it at any cost. No. I can't take such hatred from my father. Yes, I'm sure about it. I choose my family over Rehan.

8.11.2011

We came back to Indore. I couldn't face him on the flight. It feels like death to avoid Rehan. He's calling me since morning. I can't tell him. No. God, kill me please. This is getting so hard.

12.11.2011

I can't sleep. I can't even eat properly. All I do is think about not being with him anymore. He has called me over a thousand times in the last four days.

30.11.2011

I never wanted this to happen. I didn't know he was waiting for me outside my hostel. He took me to the park nearby. I tried so hard to keep my emotions in check. It was killing me every second. Then, he asked me whether I loved him or not. For one second, I thought of forgetting about my dad and telling him the truth. But then reality struck me. I did the one thing—which I had never ever imagined in the worst of my dreams. I said 'No.' I stood there for a moment to see him collapse on the ground. He fell down on his knees. That was it. I couldn't take it anymore. I walked away. I cried and cried. I didn't stop crying since then. I am still crying. How could I do this to him?

2.12.2011

At the airport. Leaving for the winter vacation. Today, I came by myself. I miss him. I don't know whether I'll be able to get over this or not. It's getting worse day by day.

9.01.2012

It's been a week since college has started but I've not seen him once. He's not come to college yet?

14.02.2012

Today, I learned from one of his friends that he dropped out of college. What have I done? I can't forgive myself for this. I go to the canteen and I see him. I walk in the evening and I see him. I go to the movies and I feel him sitting beside me. I miss him.

30.11.2012

There is not much to share. My days pass like every other. But I felt like sharing this. It's been a year now. He's still there, in my heart, not ready to leave.

16.04.2013

Today, I feel like cursing myself. I feel so bad about myself. You know what my dad said when he woke up in the ICU? "I'm sorry Riya. I was blinded by the society rules to see your love and freedom. Forgive me. I've learned my lesson." He gladly welcomed Riya and Aditya to our family. Today I'm missing

Rehan more than ever. I wish him to be here. I don't have any strings on my legs today. I'm free to choose. How dumb was I to take that silly decision?

20.05.2013

Rehan has changed his number. He's not active on any social media. I don't know how I will ever get to meet him.

18.01.2016

I met him today. After five years. I couldn't help but remember the past again. I didn't have the nerve to talk to him. But I have to tell him everything. So I gathered all my courage and asked him to meet tomorrow. He gave me his card to call him. It seemed weird to collect a card for a phone number from the person you love the most but given the fact that you have ditched the same person mercilessly in the past, it only seems fair.

I don't know but I will give him a call.

19.01.2016

I've called him twice but he didn't pick up. I guess I will just drop a message.

He replied to my message. He is coming to meet me. I'm scared. How am I going to start? I don't know. I guess I'll keep you close to me.

20.01.2016

I'm in Rehan's apartment. I think he brought me here yesterday when I passed out. He is sleeping on the couch. Such a gentleman.

Someone named Tulika has called on his phone. Is she his girlfriend? I don't know.

It all happened because of me. Rehan is in the hospital because of me. I shouldn't have gotten mad and rushed out of his apartment. I felt so small when I learned that I've expressed my love to the person who is already with someone else. I feel so bad about myself. I'm making his life miserable. I should leave. Yes. I have got to move on. We both will be better off this way.

This was the last entry. Tulika closed the diary and placed it on the table. She stared out at the sky through the window, as she thought about what she had just read. She was drawn into the story—so much so that, even after closing the journal, her mind resided in it. She was surprised by the fact that Rehan had never mentioned this part of his past to her. He kept all this a secret. Tulika and Rehan had been staying together for two years by then. They talked to each other about everything but he had never mentioned this. At first, Tulika was emotional. Her heart was moved by Kavya's tragic journey. She understood her regret, her pain and love. For a moment, she was ready to let Rehan go for Kavya. Then, another side of her character came out: Possessiveness.

"No," she whispered to herself and put the journal in her bag. She would destroy it. She never wanted Rehan to read it. She crossed out the thought of letting Kavya have Rehan. Why should she do that? She also loved him. She had supported him when there was no one else. She had given him the job, she had brought him to Mumbai, she had made him what he was. If it was not for her, Rehan Mirza might have been just another lost name. She had done everything she could for him. Not just because she could—because she wanted to.

Secondly, she could never let Rehan go. Rehan, who had also changed her in many ways. He had made her quit smoking. She didn't go to the pubs anymore; she focused on her career; she became a responsible person. She shut out all her thoughts and sat there silently. Then, she put her hands on Rehan's and dozed off.

A few hours later, she felt a movement. She woke up. It was eleven at night. She saw Rehan's fingers moving inside her palm. She held them and said, "Rehan." He was still asleep. He slowly moved his head to his left. His lips were moving. Tulika was happy to see Rehan wake up. She took his hand out of hers, and was about to call the nurse when she heard Rehan uttering something. It wasn't clear at first but the second time, she heard it clearly.

"Kavya…"

Have you ever seen a house of cards? It doesn't matter how big it is—if you pull out one card, the house collapses then and there. That one card is enough to topple the whole structure.

That one word from Rehan changed everything. All the feelings Tulika had for him were shadowed by disappointment. The flower of love that she had worshipped for so long was being stripped, petal after petal. Like a giant wave, that word washed away her little sand palace. She couldn't believe that she was going to propose to a man who belonged to someone else. She laughed at her destiny. She understood that she couldn't change anything. Maybe that was why Rehan had never expressed any feelings towards Tulika. Were there any feelings at all? She didn't know. She only knew that it was not her that Rehan wanted. She might have made a lot of difference in his life but she couldn't be a part of his life in the way she wanted.

She couldn't stay. If she stayed, she would die from the resentment. She didn't want to ruin their friendship. She didn't want to face him when he woke up. She took her bag, kissed Rehan on his forehead and, with teary eyes, bid adieu to him.

She walked out to the nurse. "Ma'am, Rehan is getting back to his senses. You might want to check on him once."

"Okay," the nurse replied.

"One more thing, ma'am. Can you please call the lady who was here before? She might have left her contact on the form."

"Sure," the nurse said.

The nurse called Kavya and told her that Rehan was waking up, and that she should come back to the hospital as Tulika had left due to some emergency.

Tulika thanked the nurse and walked out.

From the hospital, she went straight to her apartment. All through the way, her eyes did not stop shedding tears. She wasn't just leaving Rehan—she was leaving the city as well. She picked up some of her things from her room, and went to Rehan's room. She saw his table—she remembered how they used to play cards and have drinks there. She saw his camera, with which he used to take funny pictures of her. She looked at the sofa, where they used to sit and watch movies together. The memories came rushing back. She couldn't hold back her emotions—they came gushing out as tears. She stood there for a few minutes before she said goodbye.

She didn't understand why life mocked her in this way. She had been doing well on her own. She had been alone but she was happy. Yet, that didn't suit destiny, so it brought Rehan into her life. It gave wings to the bird that was content to walk on the ground. The bird learned to fly. It flew across the seas, as the sky was her new home. Just when she was getting used to her feathers, destiny laughed and clipped her wings.

While she was leaving for the airport, with a heavy heart and moist eyes, she wished she had never met Rehan.

Meanwhile, Kavya reached the hospital. She ran to the ward. She was so desperate to see Rehan wake up that she hadn't even changed out of her pajama and t-shirt. The nurse took her into the cabin. While they were walking, Kavya asked, "Where did she go?"

"I don't know, ma'am. She said she'll come back in the morning."

Kavya entered the cabin. She saw that Rehan was sitting on the bed, propped up against the backrest. She smiled.

"I'm sorry Rehan. It all happened because of me," she said.

"No. Nothing is your fault, and nothing ever was. It was always the situation that played with us," Rehan said, smiling. He held Kavya's hands. "I love you, Kavya," he said slowly. "You know, when I was hit by that car and was about to pass out, I begged God for one chance to tell you this. I've always loved you Kavya and I always will."

Kavya was confused. As far as she had guessed, Tulika was supposed to be Rehan's girlfriend. She couldn't help but ask, "What about Tulika?"

"What about her?"

"I thought…"

"No. Tulika is a very good friend. Where is she, by the way? She was supposed to come back today."

Kavya felt relieved. "She'll come. Don't worry."

…then, few days after I reached my cousin's place, I found your journal in my bag. At first, I thought of throwing it away. For some reason, I didn't. I kept it safe for a special day to gift it to you.

You deserved one more chance, Kavya. So did Rehan. Fate had been cruel to you both. I did not find another Rehan but I found someone else, and I am happy now. You both are soulmates. I wish you guys a lifetime of happiness. Keep the diary safe. And don't say anything to Rehan about this. Let this be our little secret. A big hug.

Stay blessed.

Love,

Tulika

A tear rolls down Kavya's cheek and falls on the letter. She looks at me; her eyes are red and moist. I gently pat her shoulder and tell her not to cry. Rehan may find out—which Tulika never wanted.

I congratulate her, and start to walk down the stage, when I hear Kavya saying something to me: "After leaving the hospital, we searched for her everywhere. Rehan kept calling her for days. We inquired at her office but came to know that she had resigned. We didn't have any leads left." She pauses and continues, "Rehan lost a friend. He missed her every day, though he never talked about it. He still misses her. I never had a chance to meet her personally. How is she?"

"She is good," I say.

"Where is she?"

On hearing this question, my heart skips a beat. I don't know what to say. Tulika's face comes to mind. I remember the first time I met her.

That night, after leaving the flat, Tulika boarded a flight to Delhi. She was going to her cousin's place. She was sitting quietly at the window seat, lost in thought. My seat was right next to hers.

"She is in the US with her cousin," I tell Kavya.

I start walking down from the stage. I turn and look at Kavya. She's still holding the letter, close to her heart. I turn around and walk away.

I lied. What else could I have done? Should I have told her the truth and ruined the most important day of her life? If the tables were turned, Tulika would have never done the same. Maybe that's why she never wanted Kavya to know the truth.

She lived her whole life fighting the odds, living up to her dreams and helping others. She helped Rehan when he was helpless. How hard is it to turn down a complete stranger? But she didn't. She never did anything wrong to anyone. She was a pure soul. No wonder she was blessed with cancer. As they say, the best of us don't stay for long down here.

Love is the most beautiful feeling in the world. The strongest of bonds. True love is hard to find, yet some of us do. Then, it feels as if your life becomes complete. All your pains are gone. Thirst and hunger no longer bother you. You float in a newfound heaven, like a fairy tale come to life. The air smells richer, the colors look even more vibrant and everything feels a bit livelier. You start to get comfortable in this new lifestyle, confident that nothing bad could ever happen to you.

That's where you are mistaken. Alas, life is not so simple. Before you know it, you are standing at a crossroad.

Sometimes, the love we choose doesn't choose us. We are so blindsided that we don't stop to think about whether the person feels the same way about us or not. Reality hits you like a ton of bricks when you are separated from your love. You realize that there were no flowers blossoming or trees waving, like you had imagined. Everything was just an illusion. You get scared and start to run, hoping to get away from this harsh truth. You try to fight back, to get what was yours. Sometimes, you win, and, sometimes, you lose. When you lose, everything seems to be on fire. You scream, heartbroken and angry.

However, life moves on. As your wounds heal, you give yourself a second chance, and start searching for love again. And, finally, you meet someone special. Someone who brings the life back in you. Everything becomes good and you feel whole again. You think that maybe, just maybe, everything will turn out all right. If only our lives were so predictable.

Life never ceases to surprise you. Sometimes, our past comes back to haunt us, trying to steal the newfound happiness. Does it ask us whether we are ready or not? Nope.

That is life. Unfair. Cruel. Yet, some of us find the tiny ray of hope in the darkness, and keep moving regardless of the setbacks. People give everything to life but life sometimes repays them with nothing. Still, that doesn't stop them from stepping ahead. Brave are those souls who keep walking and walking until they fade into the nothingness.

Sometimes, I wonder: What if Rehan had never met Kavya? Or Kavya had never broken up with him? Rehan would never have met Tulika, and she would have never had to leave him. Everything would have been just normal—or different. If Kavya hadn't broken Rehan's heart, he wouldn't have become successful. If Rehan hadn't said Kavya's name in the hospital, Tulika would never have called her back. If she had never left the hospital, I would never have met her.

In every story, there is a twist—which sets us up for another story. Everything is linked—not just by coincidence but by love.

What if Kavya and Tulika's lives were swapped? What do you think would've happened?

Lightning Source UK Ltd.
Milton Keynes UK
UKHW040651180119
335790UK00001B/175/P